Tied to the Tycoon

Chloe Cox

ISBN: 1481131087
ISBN-13: 978-1481131087

DEDICATION

To anyone who ever gave me a book, even if it was just to get me to be quiet.

CONTENTS

A quick note...

I can't seem to stop making my characters do these crazy things. I suppose that's what fiction is for in a lot of ways, right? I told one of my friends what these two get up to in Chapters 16-17, and she said, "well, my reaction is a combination of 'OMG lol' and 'um that's really hot,' so I definitely want to read about it."

That pretty much sums up my thoughts, too. If you're interested in ropes and rigging and such, this is maybe not totally realistic. At least if you don't want to get arrested. Also! This stuff requires a lot of training and such, which I don't really go into in the book. Jackson's done that, been there. Ava doesn't know how good she has it. ;)

About Jackson and Ava: I really, really love this couple. They are both more messed up than I thought they'd be, even though I know that makes little sense coming from the author. I just love that they try so hard for each other, no matter how dysfunctional or damaged or screwed up they are, they just...somehow find it worthwhile to try for each other, and they come through because of it. I love them for that.

I hope you do, too. :)
Chloe

chapter 1

Jackson Reed hadn't always been a gambler. Well, maybe he had. But if so, it was just one of many parts of himself that he'd worked hard to hide from the rest of the world. In the past, he'd considered it his responsibility not to play with risk, not to toy with the emotional ups and downs that risk demanded. Not because he was afraid of what the world might do to him if he lost, but because he'd always been afraid of what he might do to the world.

Well, not anymore. And he had one person to thank for that.

He sipped his bourbon, rolling the fire on his tongue and savoring the burn. It helped to focus him. Not that he really needed it; when he got like this, Jackson had the specialized perfection of an apex predator. And he was at the end of a hunt. A long, long hunt. The rest of the world would fall away, and all that would be left would be...her.

He knew he was being antisocial, standing on the fringes of the great room at Volare NY, nursing a bourbon and simply watching. He also knew no one would care. A casino night-themed engagement party at Volare NY, where most of the table stakes were of the carnal variety, meant no one gave a damn what Jackson Reed or anyone not wagering their bodies or their services did. Besides, a casino night in the middle of Christmas party season was like an unexpected oasis of actual fun. So the hanging lanterns sparkled, the champagne flowed, the live orchestra played a few torch songs, and the women laughed while the men watched with hungry eyes.

Jackson smiled, shaking his head. He didn't know many of these people very well, having cut down on his visits to Volare when his growing company demanded it. Which was why he'd had no idea that Stella Spencer had taken a job as a hostess, or that she'd fallen in love with one of the members and was apparently getting hitched. When he'd finally heard the news—where had he heard it? He didn't pay much attention to that kind of thing; he guessed it had been Lillian who had told him—he'd recognized the name immediately, and it had meant only one thing to him. He wouldn't have recognized Stella Spencer's face, he couldn't have told you anything about her at all, except for that one thing: she had been friends with *her*, in college. And so there was a chance that *she* would be here, at this engagement party, at a legendary sex club.

The woman he thought about every day. The woman he owed *everything*. The woman he hadn't seen in the flesh in almost ten years.

That was all he'd needed to know.

He'd called his brand new publicist—the one everyone had insisted he needed ahead of his new product launch—and demanded that she get him an invite. "This is the only thing I'll ask you to do, Arlene," he'd said. "And if you can't do it, find me someone who can."

It hadn't been a problem. Jackson Reed, founder and CEO of ArTech, artistic patron and tech wonder boy, now rated in the same social circles as the billionaire sheikh groom. Wasn't that a scream? The publicist had made one call to Roman Casta at Volare and it was done. Jackson hadn't told anyone the real reason for his interest, and he was surprised that Roman hadn't asked—Roman had always been sharp. But fuck it. None of that mattered now. He didn't give a damn if they threw him out, so long as he found her.

And just as he killed his bourbon, he saw her. Standing there on the other side of the room, silent and unmoving in this swirling, drunken celebration, arms folded up around her like a wounded bird. She was wearing something thin that draped over all the right parts of her beautifully, reflecting shimmering shards of pale blue at him in the dim light, and her hair, piled atop her head in some artistic arrangement, was already starting to come down and frame her face. Her face. Christ, he hadn't seen...he hadn't been prepared to see her face again. He felt weak. Looking at her was the only time he could abide feeling weak. He couldn't help but marvel at her, the perfect symmetry, their connection still unbroken, after all these years—even here, totally ignorant of his presence, she matched him: present, but standing apart. He stood apart because he had a singular purpose. But what kept her apart? What kept her standing on the sidelines, the discomfort evident in every line of her body?

This was something he'd remembered, too, from that one all-important senior year at school, when she'd transferred in. She had this impenetrable mask of cool, of charm, of flirtatious wonder, the beauty who could make anyone who talked to her feel interesting, and important, and like they belonged right there, talking to a woman who looked like that. Sometimes it seemed like he was the only one who could tell it was a mask at all. But he'd lived for the moments when the mask slipped, or those precious few nights when she took it off in his presence and was just herself. All awkward, shy, wounded, thoughtful, funny, and frightening intelligence. And eyes. Those beautiful blue eyes that could see everything, whether she wanted them to or not. She didn't, for the most part, let people know that she could see most of the things that they tried to hide. On one of those nights, she'd explained it to him: she couldn't help it, she'd said, she was perceptive, but it was kind of rude in a way. People needed their fictions. They needed their defenses.

She almost never let her defenses slip. And she almost never let them down voluntarily, not all the way. And then, the one night when she did...

Well, he was here to make up for that now, wasn't he? He was here to repay her for everything she'd given him, whether she knew about it or not.

He put his glass down and tried to think of the best way to approach her. She would be wary, the way she was now, like a hunted animal. And he didn't like how uncomfortable she looked. It had been ten years; he'd have thought she'd have a different reaction to a place like Club Volare by now. There was something that he hadn't accounted for.

But then he watched it happen right before his eyes: she assembled herself. The version of herself that most people saw. She stood up straight, held her body like a dancer who'd never known injury and only knew how good it felt to move. Her eyes flashed. Her face became that mask. It was like watching someone put on a beautiful suit of armor, and it both impressed him and made him sad.

And then he watched her walk over to the baccarat table.

The baccarat table with the very unusual stakes and several very interested looking men sitting around it, like a waiting pack of wolves.

He put his glass down and moved out into the crowd.

~ ~ ~

Ava Barnett had just started to find her old, familiar groove, holding court amongst these elite men she didn't know, holding them all in the palm of her hand and far away from anything that really mattered to her, when the stranger sat down in the darkness across from her and ordered the rest of the table to clear off. Except he wasn't a stranger, even if she couldn't see him well enough to place him—she *knew* she knew him. Yet, on what planet would she forget a man who moved like that?

On what planet would she forget a man who simply sat down and said, "Clear off," and people actually did it?

Ava herself had started to get up, an instinctual reaction to that tone of voice, when he'd stopped her. "Not you," he'd said. "Sit."

And she had done that, too, and had been irritated at herself for it. Irritated, a little turned on, and very confused.

She wished now that she could see him properly, but he was in silhouette, leaning back towards the lantern that hung behind him. She could see his hands, his large, rough, calloused hands, deftly playing with the deck of cards. The rest of him was a dim shadow, the suggestion of a square jaw, high cheekbones, and close-cropped hair reclining there with confidence. Maybe he was famous? A celebrity? That would explain this haunting familiarity, but it wouldn't explain anything else.

"Sit?" she finally said.

"We're going to play."

"Oh, we are, are we?"

"Yes."

"And who the hell are you?" she said.

He sat in silence, just toying with those cards. His fingers were little wonders, doing unconscious tricks, flipping cards, making them flutter and dance. Ava couldn't help but wonder what else he could do with those hands.

She imagined he smiled as he said, "You didn't

6

have the stake to play with those other men."

Ava narrowed her eyes. Who was this man? He spoke like he'd swallowed a bunch of gravel, or like he was trying to disguise his voice. But that was ridiculous; people didn't really do things like that. It was just that the familiarity, the sense that she knew him, was intruding on every other thought, like a persistent itch. It was driving her crazy.

Maybe it was just his manner that made her crazy. She could tell already, whoever this man was, he belonged here. He was utterly dominant.

Ava thought back over the entire, bewildering night. In context — in this absurd context — it almost made sense that some sexy, smoldering man would sit down across from her in the dark and say incomprehensible things. Of course that would happen. This was Club Volare, and so far, it had been the weirdest night in Ava's recent memory.

It had started off badly for Ava, with an unwelcome reversion to the shy, frightened version of herself that she thought she'd conquered long ago. It was just the sight of all these Doms or Masters or whatever they were, all of these good looking, wealthy men, knowing they were into BDSM and all the things Ava secretly fantasized about but hadn't had the guts to pursue in ten years. Both times she had taken that chance, it had blown up in her face. She didn't believe in fairy tales enough to think the third time would just magically work out.

So she'd wandered around this crazy fancy party, at this crazy fancy club she'd never known existed at the top of a crazy fancy hotel — and really, who expects that? A super exclusive BDSM sex club, or whatever it was, at the top of a five-star hotel? And who would have expected Stella Spencer to be into this life, of all people? Ava never would have predicted that, not in a million years, and that just added to her sense of disorientation. Ava was used to being able to read the people around her, to an almost uncomfortable degree, and now there were surprises popping up left and right. It was enough to make her question everything.

But her old friend Stella seemed happier than Ava had ever seen her. And marrying a sheikh. A *sheikh*. A sheikh who was obviously a Dom. Ava couldn't help but wonder if she and Stella might have been able to talk about this stuff, if so many things might have gone differently if Ava had felt like there was someone who understood her.

For the brief moment when she had felt like there was someone who understood her, ages ago, she'd been truly happy.

But Ava had steeled herself, determined not to think about ancient history and the exact memories of heartbreak she was trying to leave behind by coming here tonight. She was surrounded now by rich, fancy Doms, some obvious submissives, and other types she was embarrassed not to be able to recognize—and hell, it was a party. If she ever wanted to indulge her fantasies, this was the place to do it. So why was she so scared? Hiding on the outskirts of the room like a wallflower? She hadn't done that in *years*. And it was especially stupid, considering that this might be the place to secure her promotion at work, too. There were plenty of

Fortune 500 faces running around the place, and at least some of them might be in need of a new advertising firm.

But she hadn't been able to make herself mingle. It was all just too raw. Everywhere she looked, there was something that suggested sex, or bondage, or bondage *and* sex, and it all reminded her of a night she'd rather forget, and a man she'd never forget, no matter hard she tried. Funny that it didn't primarily remind her of Peter, the terrible ex she'd fled, the one who'd confused dominance with being an abusive jerk, and who she'd actually dated for a long time. Instead, it reminded her of the guy she'd spent ten years trying to get over.

Up until tonight, she'd thought she *had* gotten over him.

But she'd been frozen on the outskirts of the party, too busy grappling with her own stupid issues to enjoy herself. So, obviously, it wasn't all ancient history, and she hadn't figured it all out. So what? She'd never been a coward, either. Which was when Ava Barnett had found the strength to become the person she'd learned to be—witty, charming, gracious, beloved—and ventured out to the one thing that looked familiar: a poker table. At least she'd assumed it was a Hold 'Em table when she'd seen two cards being dealt out, and Ava knew damn well that she was good at Hold 'Em. That talent for reading people came in handy, and there'd be no better way to regain control of her night than to whip some rich guy's butt at cards.

Which was how she came to be sitting at this table with cards that didn't look like any poker cards she'd ever seen, and with a mystery man sitting across from her. A man who hadn't moved. A man whom she felt like she knew. A man whose eyes...she could *feel* them on her skin, like the gentle slide of sheet being drawn across her naked body.

Wow, Ava, do not *blush.*

She pulled herself together, remembered the arrogance of the last thing he'd said.

"What makes you think I don't have the stake to play?" she said.

"I didn't say that."

Was he being willfully obtuse? She summoned her patience, and said, "If I don't have the stake to play with them, what makes you think I have the stake to play with you?"

"You're the only one who does."

She felt him smile again. Just subtle shifts in his posture, his body language. It was like she'd known him all her life, and yet she didn't even know his name. Or what his face looked like.

Still, Ava was getting annoyed. "What the hell does that mean?"

"You don't know what the table stakes are, do you?" he said. Now she knew he was smiling in the dark. There was no disguising the amusement in his voice.

"Fine. I don't. So what are the stakes?"

He finished another shuffle and started to deal out the cards.

"You," he said.

Ava covered her surprise with a laugh. It was absurd. "Oh, really?"

"Yes. That's the nature of this table. All of those men assumed you understood that when you sat down to play. I knew that you didn't."

"You knew that I didn't? How condescending. How could you possibly know what I understand or don't understand?" The fact that he was right only made her angrier.

"Because I see you."

Ava's heart stopped. There was something in the way he said that...and that *voice*...

The man in the dark continued, "This is Volare. If you don't have chips, you bet with yourself. It's a sexual game. And you don't have chips."

"I was going to buy some."

"How many thousand dollar chips were you gonna buy, exactly?"

Ava stared dumbly at the cards that lay before her. She did not have chips, and yet, she was still in the game. She looked up, even though she knew what she would see: a stack of chips in front of the mystery man.

"I'm sorry," she heard herself say. "You are going to have to explain this to me like I'm an idiot. What, exactly, do you think I've bet?"

"You heard me," he said. "You've bet yourself."

And before she could object, the man reached out, leaning over the table, his face still in the dark, and grabbed her hand. It burned where he touched her. He pulled her toward him, raking her breasts across the table, and whispered: "One week. If I win, I can have you for one week."

Ava could scarcely breathe. She didn't know how she spoke. She knew less why she said what she did.

"And do what with me?"

"Anything I want, *Frida*."

11

Frida. The memories flooded her mind, too many, all at once, the exact ones she'd been holding at bay all night. She'd been struggling to hold up under the pressure of all those memories, and this last one, the heaviest of them all, added to the weight was just too much: *Frida.* Only one person in the world had ever called her that. Only one person in the world knew what it meant to her.

Jackson Reed.

The man she'd been trying not to think about all night.

Of course, the first memories that came crashing through all of Ava's heavily fortified defenses were the ones she'd tried hardest to forget: one incredible night together, after a long, simmering friendship, the first time she'd felt as though she didn't have to be this carefully constructed new persona, when she'd felt as though she could just be herself without danger of being swallowed up or crushed, abused or forgotten, one night when she'd confessed her fantasies to Jackson and watched him react with horror and shame, and the way he hadn't wanted to look at her…

That Jackson Reed, apparently now a member of Club Volare, was sitting in front of her, telling her she'd bet herself. Wanting a chance to win her for a week. Wanting a chance to do anything he wanted with her. Her brain almost couldn't process it. And it was only because her brain couldn't make sense of it that she said what she did. Obviously it wasn't her brain doing the talking.

"I accept," she said, and reached for the cards.

They definitely weren't poker cards.

"Do you know how to play baccarat?" he asked,

moving his chair to the side so she could finally see his face. He did look different. More confident, assured. He was still strikingly good looking, still chiseled from granite or whatever it was they said about men like him, still with that Greek god athleticism that had won him a football scholarship, but he no longer tried to hide it beneath scruffy hair and a slouched posture, like he had in college. He no longer tried to be anything. He simply was.

Wait. Baccarat?

"No." She tried hard not to sound foolish as she said it.

"You thought it was poker, didn't you?"

"Shut up."

He flashed her that grin that she'd always loved. Truthfully, she still loved it, even now.

"Then you're just going to have to trust me, aren't you?"

She swallowed. It was hard to look at him. It made her feel too many things all at once. She wasn't used to feeling so much; she'd worked hard to avoid having to do so. Jackson Reed—of all people—should see that.

"I guess so."

"Flip over your cards."

She did. She saw that he did, too. She had no idea what any of it meant.

"Now what?" she asked.

"Now," he said, that light drawl coming back into his voice, "now you're mine."

She felt her eyelids flutter. She had to look at him now. "That's it?"

"That's it. My cards total eight. You lost. You're

mine."

Ava shook her head slowly. This was all so fast, an insane confluence of events, of feelings, of memories. It was almost more likely that it was a hallucination than that it was actually happening.

He reached across the table, this time letting his savage, handsome face fall fully into the lantern light, and grabbed her hand again. His thumb caressed her skin, his fingers dug into her flesh.

"I intend to collect, Ava," he said, his grey eyes seeming to glow from within. "Starting now."

For a second, Ava felt herself melting toward him, into the desire she felt flowing around her, into the burning touch on her hand. She might have lost herself completely, simply fallen into an uncharted abyss, except that that moment of falling, of suspension, terrified her so much that it jolted her back to reality. She snatched her hand back and fled the room.

chapter 2

Jackson watched Ava run through the glittering ballroom of Club Volare like a scared rabbit and was filled not with panic or worry, but with a sense of the inevitable. Of course she'd run. Just like she had years ago, when he'd woken up to find her gone. Not just gone from his bed, but *gone*. She'd moved out of her dorm room for the final weeks before graduation, hadn't answered her phone by the time he got the courage to call, hadn't even walked in the ceremony. Maybe he'd waited too long to reach out to her, but she'd made it impossible when he finally did.

And now she was running from him again. *No,* he thought, rising from his seat with slow deliberation, *not again.* He would not let her run away *again*.

He knew Club Volare. She didn't. That much was obvious, from what he'd seen earlier. You didn't stand around like a piece of mismatched furniture if you knew where you were. There were only so many places she could go, and the security guys would tell him if she left—for a price.

And if that didn't work, well, he had money now. All that money bought a whole lot of private investigators, if it came to it.

Because Jackson Reed was *not* going to let Ava Barnett get away a second time. He owed her far too much for that. He had too many things to tell her, too many things to show her, too many things to do for her. Too many things to do *to* her.

He made his way through the increasingly buzzed couples, now all happily dancing to some kind of retro swing number, and found the door. The hall was deserted, but she'd made it pretty easy on him this time. The door to one room at the end wasn't closed all the way.

He walked to it quietly, not wanting to startle her in her hiding place. He moved the door open a silent inch and peered through. She stood by a window, the city lights from below wrapping her in a soft nimbus of filtered blue light. She held herself, her hands visible on her sides, as though she was cold or in need of comfort. He thought he saw her shoulders shake. She might have been crying.

No. He wouldn't let her get hurt again. He wouldn't let them hurt each other, wouldn't let them both spend another ten years like this. He hadn't been able to take charge of the situation back then, but he was a different man now. And he had her to thank for that. He opened the door and stepped inside.

She heard him and stiffened, but didn't turn

around. He saw one hand disappear, move to her face, probably to wipe away tears. She wouldn't want him to know that she'd been crying.

She spoke first. "I don't think this is going to work out, Jackson," she said.

"Man, can you hold a grudge," he said, advancing another step. "Ava, trust me, I'm different. What happened then—"

"People don't really change."

"Bullshit. I have." *Because of you*, he thought to himself. He didn't think it was right to say it yet, wasn't convinced that something that intense wouldn't send her running off screaming into the night. But he had to remind himself.

"Really? Since when?" she asked. Her hand was balled in a tight fist at her neck while her eyes studied the glittering skyline. He could tell she wanted it to be true, but she would take some convincing. Well, he wasn't one to beat around the bush.

"Since the last time I saw you naked."

He could actually see the shiver run up her spine in that backless dress. He was suddenly struck by the fact that he hadn't touched her in ten years. Ten years. He had waited all that time, but now he knew he couldn't wait even one second more.

He came close to her, let her feel his breath on her neck. Then he slipped his hands in the sides of that backless dress, fanning his fingers out over her bare waist and the edges of her taut belly. She shuddered, jolted a bit in surprise. Her breath hitched, and he felt himself begin to harden. He breathed in deep, and pressed his fingers into her warm flesh. He prided himself on his self-control, but Ava...

Ava made it hard.

"What would..." her voice wavered, and she swallowed. "What would the rules be?"

"You come stay with me for a week. You're mine, the entire time."

She was still tiny, compared to him. If he stretched his hands, he might just reach down far enough. It was all he could think about, how close she was to being naked. How close he was to being inside her again.

"What does that mean? I mean, are you...?" Her voice was small, uncertain. She had taken off the mask.

"I'm a member here," he said. "I'm a Dom. You'd be my submissive."

He held her close, pulling her body into his. He saw her face in the reflection of the glass in front of them and knew she was scared. Not in a mortal way, but in the way people are scared of new things, of powerful things. He wanted to dominate her—he wanted to fuck her, yes, but he wanted to wrap her in his arms, too.

"I don't really know that works," she finally said. Her tight stomach fluttered under his fingers.

"'Course you do. It's what you are."

She started to speak, but Jackson decided it was better to show her what he meant. He spun her around and pushed her up against the cool, thick glass, grabbed her thin wrists in one large hand, pinned her hands above her head, and kissed her.

She tasted just as he remembered. Sweet. Her lips were just as soft. They parted for him as he crashed into her, and Jackson Reed felt himself begin to slip under, swept away in every remembered touch, every remembered sensation of Ava Barnett. He kissed her like he might not get a chance to do it again for another ten years, and then he wanted more.

So did she. Her tongue met his, hungry as he was, and her back arched, chest pushing up towards him. He ran his fingers down her arm, the side of her face, her neck. He wasn't gentle. He pushed aside her flimsy dress and grabbed her whole breast in his hand, wanting to feel the full weight of it, all of it, his once more.

He heard himself growl.

He tightened his grip on her wrists and ran his hand down the length of her body, reminding himself of every curve. Her body reacted to his touch in shuddering waves, her muscles betraying her each and every time they made contact. He felt her come alive under his hand, her breasts, her belly, her hip, all rose, fell, breathed. Suddenly there was nothing more offensive to him than her dress, than that thin, stupid piece of fabric. He leaned down low to grab as much as he could, decided to let her keep it on at the last minute, and slipped his hand underneath instead. The skin of her thigh was hot and smooth, and when his hand found her panties, he was glad to find something he could take.

He ripped them off, vaguely aware of how absurd that was, but not giving a damn. He felt powered by some inescapable force, his momentum almost unstoppable, so close to what he'd dreamed about for years. She moaned into his mouth and raised her leg tentatively against his and he pushed on, his mouth moving to her nipple. He felt her rise against him, and then, a moment later, felt her begin to shy away. He didn't think; the most primal part of him felt her slipping away and reached out to catch her. He had her pinned against the window, and his hand was already at his belt when she pulled her hand free of his grip.

"Stop," she said, choking on her own voice.

She brought her free hand to his chest, turned her face away. He was stunned.

"What's wrong?" he said, his words pulled tight over his panting breath. His cock strained against his pant leg, and Ava…Ava…she looked so sad. Ashamed.

What had he done?

"You said it's what I am." Her own breath still came fast, and she wouldn't look at him. "But I've never done it—not properly, not the right way. Any of it. I wouldn't know where to start."

Jackson shook his head. "It's been ten years since I was a total fuckwit, Ava. In all that time, you never told anyone else what you wanted?"

"No," she said quietly.

If he'd known that was really the answer, he might not have been so incredulous. He might have been a bit more fucking thoughtful. Because in that one admission was a whole knotted, seething mass of deeper, sharper, more painful admissions, the most important of which was surely this: she'd never been that close to anyone ever again. She'd lived her life alone since then, never being fully herself.

It was worse than finding her married to

someone else. It meant he'd hurt her more than he'd imagined.

She squirmed under him, trying to get free. He held her fast.

"Ava, wait," he said. "Please. Just…ten fucking *years*."

She stopped. They were still pressed tight together, her face hovering below him, blue light creeping across her saddened cheek. All he wanted to do was make her happy. He had always been the smartest guy in the room, but now he couldn't figure out how to make the woman he'd always loved happy, even for a goddamn moment, even when he was trying. Some fucking genius.

"Is this who you are now?" she eventually said, smiling a little, trying to break the tension. "A guy who buys things? A rich guy who just…"

"I would pay to make you come," he said, without hesitation.

Her eyes grew wide.

"What?" she said.

"You heard me." He took her chin between his fingers and made sure she was looking into his eyes. "Of course, I don't have to, now that I've won you."

There was a beat before she burst out laughing, and he grinned. He could always make her laugh. He loved to make her laugh.

"Oh, shut up," she said.

"I wasn't kidding, though, *Frida*," he said softly, and she looked back up at him, the laughter gone, but the memory of it still strong, a reminder that she was safe with him. "I wasn't really kidding at all. There isn't anything I wouldn't do…"

21

He touched his fingertips to her cheek and felt his own voice cracking.

"Stop," she said. Now she struggled against him again. "Just…stop. I can't just…after all this time…"

"You owe me," he said.

There was a silence.

Finally, she said, "You can't say things like that to a woman."

"You can say it if it's true. You *owe* me," he said again, bringing her captured hand down to her side and pressing it to her lower back. With his other hand he held her face. She wasn't going anywhere. He could feel how much she liked it. "You owe me a chance to show you how much I owe you. To make it up to you."

She furrowed her brow in irritation or exhaustion, but which one, he couldn't tell.

"What the hell are you talking about, Jackson?"

He didn't answer her, not right away. Slowly he dragged his hand down her body, to the side of her right hip, where his fingers began to pull up her dress, inch by excruciating inch. He bent his head to hers, both of them quiet, waiting. The dress rose. Soon it was bunched in his hand, her leg bare.

He wanted to tell her, *you owe me because you're mine, because you belong to me, because it's only fair if I have to belong to you, because you made me what I am.* He wanted to claim her right there, make her his, the way she was supposed to be. Christ, he wanted her. And he could have her now, he knew it, *knew* he could drive her to the point where she screamed 'yes', where she would beg him to come inside her. And knew just the same that if he did it that way now, she'd wake up regretting it. She'd second-guess herself. And he didn't want that. He wanted her to *know*.

She'd never know the self-control it took not to spread her leg and slam full into her against that bright, clear window, to hear her scream as he filled her, to feel her tighten and close around him.

Instead he let the dress fall back over his hand, smoothed his palm over her hip, ran his thumb over the ridge of bone that flared out from her pubis. He savored it. Then he slipped his hand between her legs, and heard her groan.

"I know what I am now, Ava," he said, running his fingers along the length of her. She was already so wet, before he'd even parted her lips. "And I know what you are. I can show you what you are, if you'll let me."

She shook her head, but lifted her hips and slid her leg up his, hooking it around him. She had spread herself for him, but it was like she didn't know how to feel about it.

"Jackson..."

"You don't have to think about it," he said gruffly, slowly circling the entrance of her vagina with his finger. "You don't even have to think at all, if you don't want to. This whole week, I'll be in charge. I'm in control. I'll take care of you. You don't have to think about what anyone else will think. No one else has to know..."

He realized he was pleading with her. He leaned his forehead into hers, silently begging, and drove two fingers deep into her. She gasped, and a little moan escaped her throat. She kept moaning, low and soft, and he suddenly needed to see her face while she did it. He reached back up, letting her hands free for the first time, and threaded his fingers through her expensive hairstyle. When he pulled her head back, her lips were parted and her eyes were wide, limpid pools that seemed to pulsate in time with his thrusts.

He curled his fingers then, stroking her from the inside. She quivered against him and her eyes half-closed.

"No," he said, swirling his fingers and rubbing his palm into her clit. "Look at me."

He jerked her head back again, gently, and said it again. "Look at me, Ava."

She did. She looked desperate.

"Jacks, please…"

He almost hated to say it, but he had to. He had to make sure she knew. "You're not the only one with regrets. You're mine, Ava Barnett, whether you know it or not. I'm going to have you. You *will* come for me now, and you will come to me later, and you will submit."

And then he curled his fingers around as far as they would go, his thumb rubbing her wet clit in fast, tight little circles, and twisted inside her until she came for him, quaking over his hand.

He kissed her again, and wished he could go on kissing her. Instead he waited until she was done shaking, until he was sure she could stand on her own two feet. Then he smoothed the hair on her head, kissed each closed eyelid once, and murmured, "One week, Ava. No strings."

He gave her his card, and left.

chapter 3

Ava Barnett arrived home feeling like she didn't
know what. She had no frame of reference for
something like this. Like she'd been in a boxing
match, maybe? Twelve rounds or whatever it was.
Maybe, but honestly, that seemed preferable right
now to whatever this was. She felt drugged.
Hypnotized.

Ensorcelled?

She couldn't decide on a metaphor. First had
been the avalanche of memory and emotion upon
seeing Jackson Reed again, right when she'd been
trying her hardest to forget him. It had been like
one of those great seismic events that moves giant
slabs of earth and grit and mud around to reveal
something unexpected and terrible buried
underground. Then he'd just plowed right through
her and turned her inside out. Like someone had
broken into her house and emptied every single
one of her drawers, then gone outside and

unearthed something awful on her lawn.

Except that didn't make any sense either. She was totally disoriented. She didn't have a house, or a lawn. She had a crappy apartment in Alphabet City of dubious safety, the only place close to work where she could afford space for her secret painting studio. She did, however, feel that something terrible and frightening had been irrevocably revealed. *That would be my stupid issues*, she thought grimly, tossing her keys on the dining room table and kicking her high heels clear across the room. That's what the bastard had unearthed. Every damn thing she'd been working hard to bury for the past ten years.

She didn't really mean to call him a bastard. When she closed her eyes and concentrated, she could still feel him on her. And she didn't want to shower, even though she should, because she knew she'd smell him on her skin.

Ridiculous.

It wasn't just that Jackson Reed had reappeared out of nowhere; it was that he'd reappeared out of nowhere exactly as she'd always wanted him to: as a strong, sexy Dom. And apparently a wealthy one, too. How often did that happen? How often did someone actually rise beyond one's expectations and meet one's hopes?

Well, let's not get carried away. If experience had taught Ava anything, it was not to trust people who were too good to be true.

She wished she could stop thinking about him. About what he'd said. *You will come to me. You will submit.*

Ava called her voicemail and put her phone on

speaker. Three new messages. She got excited for a second before she remembered she hadn't given Jackson her phone number; he'd given her his card. With an address.

Right, because she was coming to him.

The annoying, vaguely British robot lady recording droned on about voicemail from her phone as Ava slipped out of her dress. There had been a moment, when he'd pressed her against the window, when she'd thought he would rip it clear off. And she'd wanted him to.

She stood still for a second, stark naked in her bedroom, and let the ghost of that orgasm rush through her once more. Just thinking about it, about his hands on her, *in* her, she could almost...

"Ava, it is I, your favorite." Her boss's nasal voice intruded on her thoughts. Damn, she'd told Alain about the engagement party. He'd been *very* interested in such an exclusive event. "I am a little disappointed you did not call tonight, but I am sure you did well and got many new contacts, yes? I am out late, call. Perhaps we meet up."

Ava grimaced. She spent almost as much energy deflecting Alain's creepy advances as she did doing her actual job. She was beginning to suspect that he was demanding that she land a big new advertising account before the end of the year mostly as an excuse to give her another option when she failed to meet that impossible deadline: sleep with him.

As disgusted as she was with her boss, the thought of sex immediately brought her back to Jackson Reed. And what he could do with just his hands and a thick glass window. She still thought about that night they'd shared together, just before

27

graduation. The one night. It had given her a totally unrealistic expectation of sex; before Jackson, she'd only ever slept with two guys — one in high school, who she'd more or less shanghai'd into the experience just to get it over with, and then Peter, who had been a cheating jerk and who had been her big reason for transferring for her senior year. Jackson made her think she'd just had bad luck. Jackson made sex make...*sense*. He'd made it seem like vital necessity, like a basic human right.

Maybe she'd only convinced herself that there would be more like him because it made it easier to walk away from him. *Not walk*, she reminded herself. *Run. You ran away, and you hid.*

Not her proudest moment.

Don't think about it. She actually flinched, even though she was alone. It still made her feel ashamed, still made her feel small, all these years later.

"*Second message,*" the British robot lady voice intoned.

"Ava—"

Ava immediately recognized her mother's voice and leapt across the room to grab at her phone. She pressed madly at buttons until her mother's voice stopped.

"*Message erased.*"

Thank God. If the memory of Jackson's face could reliably make her feel ashamed, her mother's voice could do a whole lot worse with a whole lot less. Her stress response was just instinctual. There was nothing to be done about it; she just had to stand there, waiting for it to filter through her system, waiting for the fear and anger to drain away.

Ava was so damn tired of being afraid. She'd been afraid of making the final leap into being submissive, and then Jackson had found her.

He'd said one week, no strings, he'd be in charge. He'd take control and show her everything. It sounded like a free pass to explore all the sexual stuff she'd never trusted anyone else with, but was it really free? The man had already broken her heart once. And as much as she'd tried to forget Jackson Reed, in her worst moments, when she felt most alone, the memory of him had been a comfort to her, late at night. Her friendship with Jackson was the closest she'd ever felt to being safe, and cherished, and treasured. The closest she'd ever been to anyone, ever. What if it had been an illusion? What if one week with Jackson revealed that she'd been wrong all along?

"Stop thinking about Jackson Reed!" she said to the empty room. Maybe if she said it out loud, it would actually take.

She pressed a button on her phone to replay the last message. She'd missed it completely, thinking about Jackson, and fear, and being alone forever. *Good job, drama queen,* she thought, and snorted. She was glad to hear her sister's voice, finally.

"Hey, it's me. Um, don't hate me, but I'm just calling to remind you about dinner with Mom." Ava cringed. What Ellie was too sweet to say was, 'Please, for the love of God, don't make me go alone.' How could Ava let her little sister deal with that all on her own? Ellie was stuck with their mother the rest of the year, but she shouldn't have to bear the burden alone during the holidays.

"And it's Christmas, Ava," Ellie's voice said.

"And don't roll your eyes, I'm not being sweet. I just want to see you."

Ava laughed, rooting around for her pajamas. Ellie couldn't help but be sweet, even when she was trying to be a bitch. Ava tried to tell her, *you can't fight who you are*, but Ellie was a stubborn little sister.

Wait, who can't fight who they are? Ava stopped halfway through getting her pajama pants on and nearly fell over. *Did I just accidentally give myself good advice?*

Jackson had told her he knew what she really was. That he was going to show her.

She shivered.

The most infuriating thing about Jackson's offer was that it had shown her how much she was missing. The thing was, not finding anyone she could trust meant that Ava hadn't been able to be fully herself—ever. She couldn't fully be herself at her job, she couldn't fully be herself with her family, she didn't even feel like she could share her painting anymore, which she did in secret in a tiny little second bedroom in her apartment. But this was something there was no outlet for. This was sex. And the kind of sex where she definitely needed someone else to be there.

And it hadn't been an offer so much as an order.

Which was damn sexy.

And he'd called her *Frida*.

"Damn it!"

She plopped onto her bed, her comfy pajama pants still half around her ankles. She was always telling Ellie not to fight who she really was, and yet Ava had been doing that for ten years. At least. She was still doing it. The universe had gone ahead and plonked the best man she'd ever known in her lap, and he had told her he wanted to fulfill all of her fantasies for a week, and her reaction was…to freak out? Who does that?

Maybe she was just rationalizing the fact that she couldn't stop thinking about him, that she felt an inescapable pull whenever she remembered his hands on her body, as though there were an invisible cord that tied her to him. Maybe it was that she'd never wanted anyone so badly in her entire life. Maybe it was that he'd said that she belonged to him.

She knew from experience what it meant to trust Jackson Reed with her heart, and she wasn't about to do that again. But she'd never had the chance to trust him with her body. Until now.

It was almost like she didn't have a choice.

It's ok, Ava. No strings. Just sex.

She grabbed her running shoes, coat, and purse, and ran out the door before she could change her mind.

chapter 4

Jackson Reed did his five-hundredth sit-up, lay back, sweating, and waited.

Fuck.

It hadn't worked. He'd had at most a moment's respite before his dick demanded access to a woman who wasn't there. He'd been like this all goddamn night, ever since he'd left Ava Barnett breathing hard in an empty room.

He flipped over and punched out quick twenty chest-to-deck push-ups, then switched to one-handed when the burn wasn't enough. *Might never be enough.* It was out of character for Jackson to vacillate like this—or at least it had been for a long time. Realizing how damaged Ava had been had thrown him. He'd hurt her more than he'd known, years ago, and then he might have done it again tonight by pushing her. Jackson worked hard not to be a man who hurt people, not to be a man who pushed people past where they ought to go just to show he could. Not to be a bully, not to be...

He worked very hard not to be like *him*.

The idea that he'd become what he feared in the very process of trying to become the opposite, like some stupid Greek myth, angered him.

Where the hell is she? he thought, sitting up, the sweat dripping down his chest. He was sure she'd come — as sure as he'd ever been of anything. They still had that connection. He'd seen it in her eyes when she came all over his hand.

He felt himself getting hard again, and groaned.

The thought of her, *any* thought of her, was enough to get him going. She'd tripped some wire, set off some sort of damn fuse left over from ancient history, and now he was like a caged bull.

It made it hard to think. And Jackson had a lot to think about.

He had to think about how much he didn't know about Ava Barnett. He was willing to bet he knew more than most — maybe more than anyone, the way she kept herself closed up tight. But that didn't mean much. He knew she must have been rubbed raw already, even more so than he'd thought, a woman who'd already been battered by the world, or maybe just some of the people in it. She had to be, if the one metaphorical blow from Jackson that stupid night was enough to knock her out for the count for ten years.

He thought back and tried to remember details from the late nights they'd stayed up after studio sessions for their shared art class. Details were hard. He remembered the vague outlines of a relationship that went bad for her just before she'd transferred in at the beginning of senior year, a relationship she'd never wanted to talk much about. And he remembered the way she had mostly changed the subject whenever anyone had brought up family, but half the time, Jackson'd been right behind her, no more eager to talk about his family than she had been to talk about hers. And they were both scholarship kids, both of them working outside of class. But it was difficult to recall the hard facts of her life before him, because that's not how he thought of her. She wasn't a dry biography or a cold psychological profile. Every time something useful started to float to the surface, there'd be something else, something of far more interest. Her laugh, or the way she smirked at him at a party, sharing some private joke. The look she got on her face when she was listening to someone else's problems, like there was nothing more important in the world than whatever was making her friend sad. All those things you notice when you're in love.

Goddamn it.

He'd just been too self-absorbed, too concerned with his own bullshit. She'd been too good at hiding. And they'd both been too enamored at that connection they'd felt to do much more than enjoy it. And he'd let her slip through his fingers because of it.

There was, of course, the one night he remembered in crystal clear detail, one night he'd carried with him since then, and would until the day he died. The night she had given him the two most precious gifts he'd ever gotten.

You owe her.

That was all that was important. He couldn't just wait around, hoping she'd come to her senses. He'd waited ten years to become a man who was good enough for her, and he wasn't going to fuck it up by waiting around any longer. He wasn't going to give either of them a shot at ruining their second chance.

Jackson jumped up, possessed with purpose. He was going to go out there and find her; there was just one thing he needed to hide first. No point in scaring her when he did finally bring her back here.

He barely had time to find a hiding place before the doorbell rang.

chapter 5

As soon as Ava's finger touched the stupid bell—which, this was the only door in New York with an actual bell on it, wasn't it? Of course it was—as soon as she did the one thing that was completely irrevocable, she was beset by doubt. Not when she'd given the cab driver the wrong address, twice, in her nervousness; not when she'd stumbled into Jackson's swanky lobby, all ready to give the doorman some crazy story, and had simply been waved through because he assumed she must have gotten locked out while feeding a meter or something; not when she realized in the elevator, *Oh, hey, I'm wearing pajamas, a winter coat, and running shoes, and it's two in the morning, what the hell am I doing.* Only when she'd actually rung the bell in the middle of the night, surely waking up the man she'd come to see, had she remembered to doubt herself.

Well, not just any man. Jackson freaking Reed.

She was about to turn around and slink away when the door opened wide to reveal Jackson, shirtless, sweaty, in low slung pajama bottoms.

Oh God.

She opened her mouth, but no sound came out.

"Come in," he said. It didn't sound like an invitation. It sounded like an order. Ava was grateful for the direction. The sight of him had just leveled her.

She obeyed.

His apartment was dark, except for one area right by a couch in a corner, where there were a few dumbbells and other exercise-looking things strewn about in a pool of lamplight. She couldn't see much else, but she could see that while he might not have been asleep, she had definitely interrupted something. She was just turning around to apologize and explain when Jackson grabbed her by the waist and kissed her.

He did more than that. He pressed her whole helpless body against his, wrapped his arm around her like a vice, grabbed her hair, and took her mouth with his. He was hard against her. His cock pushed into her belly as he sucked on her lower lip, and every muscle in Ava's body gave out. The tension and doubt rippled and left her, as though he had sucked it right out of her, and now she only craved more contact. Her chest rose, her breasts trying to reach his chest, and her hands ran up and down his shoulders and back, feeling the muscles and the sweat that was already starting to cool. In one stroke, he smoothed his hand down her neck, to her breast, her belly, her hip, her ass, and then he pulled away, leaving her gasping.

There was a hint of a smile in his grey eyes.

"That said it better than whatever you were going to say would've done, didn't it?" he said.

She nodded and looked down. She couldn't help herself. He looked huge, bulging through his pajama bottoms. She remembered him as big, but...damn.

He said, "I'm glad you're here."

"Me, too." Her voice sounded hoarse.

"If you hadn't shown up, I was going to have to come out and find you." He pulled her peacoat down over her shoulders. His hands brushed her bare arms, and she jumped. Now she had on only a tank top and her own pajama bottoms.

Ava was feeling woozy, being around him, and she fought it. She desperately wanted to keep the conversation in the realm of the sane. Somehow, every interaction between them threatened to veer into crazytown almost immediately, and Ava was suddenly feeling like she needed to keep her wits about her. This was more troubling than she'd thought. She wasn't just feeling lust; she was feeling...she was *feeling*.

"How were you going to come and find me?" she asked. She tried to sound nonchalant, but her voice shook anyway. "You don't even know where I live."

He looked at her, completely serious. "You know I would find a way."

She felt herself crumbling, felt her senses leaving her, felt... No. She couldn't fall already. Whatever it was between them had short-circuited her brain, wired itself directly to her gut, her heart. This was the power of the man: he made her forget everything she'd promised herself.

He moved closer and slipped his hands under her tank top, resting them for a moment on her bare skin, preparing to take the top off. She inhaled and fought through the pulse roaring in her ears.

"Wait," she whispered.

Please don't make me say it again, she thought. *I don't think I could say it again.*

He bent his head toward hers and traced the line of her jaw with his finger. She could smell him, musky and strong. It did not make her resistance easier.

"We should talk first," he finally said.

She exhaled with relief and nodded. Not just because she needed talk, but also relief that he was still just as sensitive as she remembered. That connection was still real. She was right to feel safe, and as soon as she felt that, the words just came tumbling out.

"How does this work? I mean…what are the rules? I have no idea, I've never…like, I mean, are there safewords? What happens if—"

Lightning quick, he snaked his arm around her back, reached down, and grabbed her ass hard enough to shut her up. He pulled her up toward him, his fingers slipping into the fold between her buttocks. Her clit screamed, and her whole body heard it.

He said, "Slow down."

It's not as if she had a choice. There was hardly any oxygen going to her brain.

He began to caress her up and down with his free hand along the length of her body, almost petting her. It made her both calm and incredibly...the opposite of calm. Whatever that was. She could barely think.

"Yes," he said, his hand grazing her breast, "you'll get a safeword. Something you'll remember, but something that won't come up otherwise. It's not something you want to get confused about. Pick one."

Ava tried hard to think of the least sexy thing she could. Must keep the boundaries. Must keep the strings. Maybe that would calm her down, make her feel in control of herself. She could almost hear her mind lurching into gear, like an old manual transmission that hadn't been lubed up in... *Oh, God, don't think about lube.*

"Garlic press?" she said, breathlessly.

He burst out laughing, his grey eyes sparkling.

"Yeah, that'll work."

His voice was soft, but he was done waiting. He let her go only to lift her arms and push her tank top up over her breasts and off her body. He threw it somewhere without even looking, his eyes focused only on her, standing half naked in front of him. He let his gaze rake her up and down like he wanted her to *know* he saw her. Her breath caught in her throat, and then he caught her by the waist again and pulled her close.

"But if you ever want to use that safeword," he said, pinching one nipple, "I won't have done my job."

Ava closed her eyes and tried to breathe. He was toying with her nipple and her breast, his iron grip holding her motionless.

"Your job?" she finally managed.

"I told you: I'm going show you what you are.

I'm going to show you that you're mine."

Ava's eyes flew open, and her heart thudded hard in her chest. She was so far gone that she couldn't tell what was lust, what was panic, and what was...something else. When she spoke, her voice sounded small.

"You said no strings," she said.

"And I meant it, *Frida*. You are mine for one week. After that, you can do what you want."

He was so close, his eyes gentle, and his hands rough. Ava kept opening and closing her hands, balling them into little fists in an effort not to use them. She wanted to touch him so badly, but didn't trust herself at all. If she didn't have ground rules, she'd fall completely.

"What does that mean, I'm yours?" she said.

"It means what I said it means. You are mine, in any way or any place I want, at any time I want. You obey my orders. You accept my discipline. You come for me," he said, squeezing her breast hard, "Over, and over, and over again."

Oh.

"No strings," she said again. "Just sex."

"No strings."

She bit her lip and nodded.

He didn't hesitate. He knelt down and stripped her pants off. Now she was completely naked. He lifted her feet out of the useless pants and slowly worked his way up. His hands inched up the backs of her legs and his mouth kissed a trail up the front. She shuddered as he got closer, closer, kissing his way up her tender thighs. His hands gripped her buttocks, and then he nuzzled his face between her legs. It was so strangely intimate, so...

She nearly collapsed. He caught her.

In one swift motion he stood, cupping her ass in his hands and lifting her up so fast she had no time to react. She spread her legs and wrapped them around his waist, as they had almost nowhere else to go. His cock, straining against his pants, pressed against her naked flesh, and she felt herself seep through the thin cotton of his pajama bottoms. She didn't have time to be embarrassed while he carried her off into the dark.

Ava gripped his neck, as though they were on some wild veldt somewhere and not a luxury apartment in the West Village, and just held on. He busted through some door she couldn't see, navigating his way in the dark, and then she was on her back, her legs still wrapped around him, his weight pressing her into a soft mattress. A bed. He ground his erection against her, and she caught her breath, grasping at his back.

"I remember," he said, and for the first time, his voice sounded choked. "I remember what you asked me for. I've always remembered."

Ava couldn't say anything. She was torn between wanting to scream yes, wanting to tell him to shut up and get inside her, and wanting to run away from the things he'd just brought up.

"You wanted to be tied up," he said roughly, unwrapping her arms from around his neck.

Ava felt her chest constrict. She did. She'd said that. She'd meant that. She still did. But it was too...

"Not yet," she whispered. "Please just get inside me."

He rumbled low deep in his chest. "Not *yet*," he

said, and pinned her wrists up above her head with one large hand. He ran the other down the length of her body again, stopping only to lift her left leg up and out, spreading her as wide as she could go. She heard the rustle of fabric, the little sounds that let her know what was about to happen, and felt her back begin to arch in anticipation. *Jackson Reed.*

He pressed his mouth to hers and sank into her.

"Ava," he said, his breath on her cheek, and he began a steady rhythm, controlled at first, but growing wilder with each beat. He filled her, more even than she'd remembered, pushing deeper with every stroke, saying her name over and over until it sounded like a chant, or a prayer. She couldn't escape, wouldn't have wanted to if she could. She wanted to be taken, completely, by Jackson Reed.

Soon she was bucking wildly against him, wanting to feel fuller, if that were possible, wanting to drown totally in him. He plunged into her with abandon, driving out all her worries, pushing aside her anxieties, and leaving room only for the swirling force that gathered in her core. He tilted her up and pistoned against her g-spot until she closed in around him like a sleeping flower and then exploded, unfolding outwards again and again, until she had nothing left.

chapter 6

It took a second for Ava to realize where she was. It obviously wasn't her apartment. The sheets were too nice, for one, and the light was all wrong, in that there was so much of it. No one she knew had windows this big.

Holy crap, that all really happened.

She buried her face in a sinfully soft pillow. She couldn't turn over and look. She knew what she'd find: Jackson Reed.

This was basically her best dream and her worst nightmare all rolled into one. That actually, really, for serious happened. Stella's engagement party. The stupid bet! The best sex of my life.

Just the thought of facing Jackson this morning, of facing everything they'd done and the way it had made her feel, put an iron knot of anxiety in her stomach. He had already been deeper inside her, both physically and metaphorically, than any man since...since him. This was terrible. Ava was in no way prepared for this kind of…

Well, saying she wasn't prepared for this kind of vulnerability sort of made her seem like not the most well adjusted person. But this was a legitimate shock. She had completely misjudged her ability to just keep it sexual, to just explore that one side of herself. She needed time to think, to collect herself, to decide what she really wanted and how she should proceed so she wouldn't get her heart broken by Jackson freaking Reed — again.

She needed to get the hell out of there.

Slowly, Ava worked her arm out from under her pillow and used it to push herself up on the bed. She could feel the weight of Jackson right behind her; she'd have to be stealthy if she were going to get out of this without waking him up and making a scene. She would come back. She would call him. She just needed to think.

But she couldn't bring herself to look at him. He'd be sleeping, looking beautiful and good, and totally unaware that she was leaving, and she couldn't face that, either.

You are thirty-two years old, Ava Barnett. You are supposed to be a grown up. Grown ups do not sneak out of beds.

She really did feel like a dumbass college student again, but it was her only option. The only one she could bear, anyway. Using every abdominal muscle she'd ever earned at the gym, she lifted her legs and swung them over the edge of the bed. She couldn't see her clothes, which, she remembered now, weren't even proper clothes, but freaking pajamas. And they were out in the other room. Perfect. She'd just get up without moving the bed, and…

Ava's dismount was perfect, but a tug on her left arm pulled her back to the bed with a definite bounce.

What the hell? And then: crap, did I wake him up?

Cringing, Ava turned to look.

And she saw Jackson Reed, one sleepy eyebrow raised, holding the end of a black leather lead that was fastened to a black leather cuff on her left wrist.

"Going somewhere?" he said, and yawned. Then he pulled on the lead, dragging her back down until she was flat on her back, her nakedness very much on display for him.

"What the fuck?" she said, and tried to sit up. Jackson put two strong arms on either side of her and kissed her back down.

When he finally let her go, she was breathless. "Not fair," she said.

He was admiring the view of her naked breasts, but apparently his mind was still working. "Neither is running away," he said.

Ava didn't have an immediate comeback. She was not prepared for him to make sense, not when he'd apparently tethered her to his bed. She looked at the cuff on her wrist and couldn't believe it.

"Seriously, Jackson, what is this?"

She held up her left wrist as much as she could while still pinned under his weight. He was making it hard for her to focus, or stay mad, or think about anything other than his body on top of hers. And by the look on his face, he knew it, too.

He pushed a knee between her legs and nudged

them wide, settling in between them like he belonged there. It felt like he did belong there. The thought sent Ava into a panic. That felt an awful lot like strings.

"What's wrong?" he said, his eyes going soft as he studied her changing face. He could read her, as always.

"What's wrong is I've woken up tied to your bed, not knowing what the hell I'm doing, or what's going on, or what any of this means, or if I'm ready for it, or even if — oh God, did we even use protection?"

"I get tested every six months."

And she was on the pill. Still, though. She ignored him. "And all I want is to go think somewhere, and —"

He kissed her again. It wasn't fair. It didn't answer any of her questions or address her concerns, but replaced her thoughts with a nameless warmth.

"Stop doing that," she said when he let her up for air. "I need to think."

"You've been thinking for ten years," he said. "How's that worked out for you?"

She didn't have an answer for that, either. At least, not a good one. His grey eyes wouldn't let her look away, and wouldn't let her hide.

"You can't keep me prisoner," she finally said, and wriggled beneath him, trying to rise. "I'm not —"

This time, he left no room for doubt. He grabbed her wrists and wrapped the long leather lead around them both, holding them above her head again. He wrapped one arm around the underside

47

of her thigh and brought it close to her chest so she could feel her spread folds wet against him, and he kissed her again, that same melting kiss. He moved his mouth down her throat while she mumbled his name, kissing his way across her chest until he took her nipple in his mouth. He sucked on it until she groaned, then abruptly pulled away.

"Then say it," he growled into her ear. "Use your safeword. Call the whole thing off, right now, and you'll never have to see me again."

Never see him again? She hadn't thought of that, hadn't wanted that. That wasn't what she'd meant. It would be the safest thing to do, though. It would. That was obvious.

She couldn't do it.

"That's not fair," she began.

"No, it's not," he said, and shifted his weight, rubbing himself against her again. She could feel herself soaking him. "It's not fair that you walked out on me, either, and never gave me a chance to try to fix it. It's not fair that you made a goddamn promise, and you're trying to walk away from it again. A lot of things in life aren't fair."

Ava felt like she wanted to cry. She also felt like she wanted to fuck, like she wanted to let Jackson Reed take her each and every way he wanted her, like she could just live in this bed with him forever, and that completely and utterly terrified her. What would she be like at the end of a week of this? She wanted this, wanted to get to be a sub, couldn't imagine it with anyone but Jackson. But what if the cost was too high?

Not that she could ever say that. She hoped he couldn't see that far into her.

But he pressed the point, like he sensed weakness. "You have a good reason you shouldn't honor the deal?"

Ava's mind was running at a million miles a minute, coming up with reasons that didn't involve revealing how she really felt. She was actually pretty good at that.

"Jackson, it's not... A week? I have a job, you know, and family obligations, and...I'm supposed to have dinner with my mom and my sister, and—"

"You can be excused for that."

Now it was her turn to raise an eyebrow. "'Excused?'"

He smiled down at her, slid his hand down her raised thigh, and looked into her eyes. Nowhere to hide, Ava. She felt a chill as he shifted to give himself access to her. With one finger he began to trace the contours of her folds. In spite of herself, her hips moved. He smiled wider.

"What part of 'mine' didn't you understand, Frida?"

That nickname again. Every time he said it, she went back to that night. Back to what he knew about her, to the person she used to be, to the person she had once thought she would become. It made her feel known and loved and also exposed and sad all at once.

His fingers made it impossible for her to articulate any of that. Not that she would have, anyway. None of that was the no-strings-sex they'd agreed on.

"Isn't this what you want, Ava?" he whispered, tugging on the lead that held her wrists. The leather cut into her skin with a soft bite, and just the knowledge that she was bound sent a delicious current down the length of her body. She couldn't deny it: she had always wanted this. Always wanted a chance…

"Yes," she said. She almost wanted to sob, but instead arched up to his hand.

"Do you trust me for this?" he asked, and looked deep into her eyes.

He knew. That was the thing—he always knew. Somehow knew that this was hard for her, knew that she had things to overcome, even if he didn't know why or what, and knew just as certainly that she needed to do this. Just as she knew now.

"Yes," she breathed. He was the only one she could trust. She could do this, and it would be like getting a do-over of the past, and then she could finally put it behind her. She could move on, confident in what she wanted.

"Yes," she said again, louder. "Yes."

He grinned down at her, his smile flashing in the morning light.

"You need to make any phone calls?" he asked.

"What?"

"You know, that job you have."

Oh God. Alain. She'd just have to tell him she was going after that big account he wanted. Not what she'd want to tell Jackson, though. "I have vacation time coming up," she lied.

"Good."

It was just dawning on her what that meant. "Twenty-four hours a day?" she said in a small voice. "You mean…"

"Twenty-four hours a day." He was smiling more now. "All access, all the time."

She swallowed.

"But what about your business?"

"My company will be just fine," he finally said. "We've got a big launch coming up, and I'll announce an IPO in the new year, but I've done what I can. I've hired people for the rest."

"You can just...do that?"

"I already have. I was wondering what I was gonna do this week. Now I'm gonna spend it with you."

That's right, she reminded herself, no strings. Their connection made it safe to do this, that was all. It didn't mean anything else. There were no excuses. Fate had essentially swooped in out of nowhere and dropped her perfect fantasy — Jackson Reed as a Dom who wanted her — right on top of her from a great height.

So why was there this nervous tension coiled tight in her middle? Because she'd gotten so used to hiding herself away that being with someone who could really see her was terrifying?

Well, that's a stupid reason.

Everything was so jumbled inside her that it was impossible to make sense of it all. She wanted to get to her studio, the tiny little half bedroom in her apartment where she still painted, furtively, in secret. That was usually when she figured things out and found a way to see the world clearly. But she couldn't just say, Jackson, you mind if I go off to a secret place I don't tell anyone about, and no, you can't come.

"Hey," she heard him say, and looked up again to find him staring into her face. "Where'd you go?"

Ava blinked, and a tear fell down the side of her face. That just made her mad. Crying? Seriously? How the hell was she supposed to explain actual tears without sounding like a crazy person?

But she didn't have to. Jackson touched the side of her face and carefully wiped away the tear. Then he said, "You're mine. It's just a week, no strings. Let go."

She took a big gulp of air and nodded.

He kissed her.

"Now open up," he said, and spread her legs even wider. "You owe me an apology for trying to sneak out."

That made her instantly wet. Wetter. He apparently felt it.

"I'm sorry," she said softly, suppressing a smile.

"Oh no, Ava," he said, and thrust into her in one bold, surprising stroke. She whimpered and arched her back into him, craving more, though she felt shockingly full. "That's not good enough. You're gonna scream it."

chapter 7

It felt wrong. Necessary, but wrong.

Jackson hadn't felt this jumpy since high school, hadn't been this nervous ever. He had lied to Ava Barnett. It was for her own good—and his, too—but he'd still lied. And immediately he'd realized all the work he was going to have to do to cover his sorry ass, and that he was going to have to do it in private, which meant some alone time, as much as he wanted to spend every possible moment with a naked Ava. The first thing he'd done after fucking Ava properly was order her into the shower.

"You're *ordering* me?" she'd said, rolling onto her side and propping her head up on one lovely hand. Her lovely breasts had been right there, too. Made it hard to concentrate.

So did her impertinent attitude. The Dom in him wanted to discipline her all damn morning. Instead, he'd just felt her up.

"You forget our arrangement already?"

She'd stuck her tongue out him. He'd had no choice but to drag her across the bed and over his knees. She'd let out a surprised laugh, like she couldn't believe how good it felt to be manhandled like that. It was all he could do not to take her again.

"I should spank you red," he'd said. "But I think you'd enjoy it too much. Get in the shower. I've got to see to plans for the rest of the day."

"Plans?"

"Just you wait and see."

"What about my clothes? I don't have any, I have to go back to my apartment—"

"I'll take care of all that," he'd said. "Consider yourself lucky, too. I'm feeling generous. Otherwise, you'd be naked the whole week."

He'd watched her beautiful, naked ass as she sauntered to his master bath, and he hadn't missed the coy look she'd thrown over her shoulder, either. She thought she was back in control after that moment of raw vulnerability in bed. That was ok for the moment. He loved both Avas. He loved the charming mask she presented to the world just as much as the woman she was underneath, because both were part of her. He just needed to show her it was safe to be herself around him all the time.

Hell, he needed to her to be around him, period. Preferably for the rest of his life.

He waited to hear the shower turn on and allowed himself a moment of thinking about her, naked, with hot water dripping down her skin. Then he launched himself out of bed and hunted down his phone. He had to make a bunch of phone calls, but the first one was not about women's clothing, or even about all the things he wanted to plan for Ava. This first phone call was not going to be fun.

"Hello, Jack."

Lillian sounded like she expected to hear from him, and like she knew exactly how the conversation was going to go, the way she always did. Which was impossible; it was an affectation, like it always was. Jackson's COO and former fling called herself a switch at Club Volare, but he'd never seen her be even a little bit submissive outside the club.

"Lillian, I need you to help me out."

"I thought something might be amiss. Your inbox is piling up. Where are you?"

"I'm at home. And I won't be coming in for the rest of the week."

There was a pause.

"You're joking."

"Something important has come up, Lil. We're just gonna have to work around it. It's only the tail end stuff, anyway."

Another pause.

When she spoke, Lillian's voice was tight. "Is everything ok?"

Jackson honestly wasn't sure what to make of that. Things had been chilly between them since they'd decided to keep things strictly professional. It had been a mutual decision, and it'd made sense, since they'd never actually been that good together—at Volare or elsewhere, outside of business. But Lillian had seemed pissed when he'd agreed too quickly.

"Everything's fine. It's a personal thing."

"I guess that means it's none of my business, then."

"Christ, Lillian."

Jackson thought he could actually hear her backpedaling.

"I didn't mean it like that, Jack. You know what you want done, and I'll send you a list of things I think can be easily delegated. I'm sure you're right that we'll find a way to manage the rest."

He gritted his teeth. It was just like Lillian to make it sound like she was doing him a favor and fully expect him to be grateful.

"I know I'm right," he said. "I'll expect that list by close of business."

"Of course."

That smooth, placating tone. If Lillian weren't the best, most competent chief operations officer in existence, he would have severed their relationship completely. He'd been a fool to get involved with her personally, though at the time it had seemed like a no-brainer—Lillian was experienced in the BDSM scene, and had offered to show him the ropes, help him get better as a Dom, no strings attached. One of his buddies had warned him that no strings *always* meant strings, but Jackson hadn't listened.

With a start, he realized he'd just told the same lie to Ava. "No strings attached." That was, of course, bullshit. There was every string imaginable. But Ava was different. Him and Ava were different. He'd tell her about those strings when she was good and ready.

"Lillian, I gotta go."

He did. He had other things to attend to. If Jackson wanted to heal whatever damage he'd done to Ava Barnett and then win her over for life, he had a lot of work ahead of him. First and foremost was showing her not only how rewarding her life as a sub could be, but how much she enjoyed it.

He had another phone call to make.

~ ~ ~

Ava took long showers. It was a weakness — she knew it. And Jackson's shower was like the shower of the gods: it had not one, not two, but three of those rainforest drenching shower heads, one directly overhead and another two on the sides, all encased in this warm tiled room that was almost as big as her secret art studio. There were actual bedrooms in New York that weren't as big as this shower.

When she finally emerged, she realized that she had lost some time. She also realized that Jackson hadn't joined her in his heavenly shower, which was probably considerate of him, but also left her with a stab of insecurity. Was he already tired of her? Maybe a whole week was just too much, and she should cut her losses and just call it off sooner rather than later. It would be devastating to have him just get bored of her. That wouldn't be as bad as getting her heart broken, but it would be pretty humiliating.

It didn't help that he appeared to be gone.

Nope, she was sure of it. She checked every

spare bedroom—*both* of them, she noted, which, in New York terms, was just absurd—the double-height living room with the corner couch she'd noticed the night before, the open kitchen with its beautiful slate countertops and bronze fixtures, even the terrace. Which, again: he had a terrace. But Jackson was nowhere to be found.

"What the hell?"

Saying it out loud did not help.

Ava dug around in the all-purpose purse she'd brought with her until she found her phone. She had a new voicemail. She'd already dialed her voicemail number before she realized that she still hadn't given Jackson her phone number. It was just another message from her boss, apparently left in the middle of the night.

"Ava, my Ava, my dear, I have some bad news," Alain crooned. He sounded tipsy. "I have spoken to the board, and there are many cutbacks and expenses next year. Don't tell anyone, yes? I don't put this in an email!"

Ava stared at her phone. *No shit you don't put that in an email. That would make it evidence.*

Alain's voice dropped to a conspiratorial whisper. "But I think I can save you, yes? If I tell them you are valuable, you bring in business, or something—whatever. Call me back, Ava, we'll chat, ok?"

So now it was bring in a new account under an impossible deadline or lose her job, not just a promotion. Or the other option: "whatever." Ava sat back on Jackson's plush black couch, wrapped in his comfy bathrobe, and tried to figure out what she was feeling. It wasn't easy. She blamed this on

Jackson. He'd shaken her to her core, and now pretty much nothing looked the way it should. Like this sudden crisis with her job: she should be totally panicked. Part of her *was* totally panicked. She'd worked hard at her advertising career; she'd worked hard at becoming the sort of woman who fit in that career. And hell, she'd even told her mother that the promotion was a lock the last time they'd spoken, just to win the argument, and now she was probably going to lose the job entirely? Fantastic. That brought up all those familiar and expected feelings of dread and worthlessnes, but there was something else, too.

Something Ava couldn't identify. But something...kind of good. A lightness. It made no sense, none at all.

This man is like a freaking drug. You're still high the next morning, Ava, get over it.

"You're not so good at following instructions, are you?"

She started. It was the man himself, standing in the open door, knocking the last bit of snow from his boots. Her insides rolled over just at the sight of him. It took a second for her brain to work again, but when it did, she was on her guard. She didn't think she could take another emotionally intense conversation. Any Serious Conversation would bring up too much stuff about a guy who was going to be gone in a week.

"What instructions?" she said.

He pointed at the slate-topped kitchen bar, the only barrier between the open kitchen and the living room. There was a piece of paper on it. A note. She'd totally missed it, but she was glad to have something to keep her busy while Jackson took all of his winter stuff off. She was feeling wary, and yet, even the suggestion of that man undressing was just...

She still felt off-balance around him.

The note did not help with that.

I've gone out. Lie down on the bed, naked, eyes closed, and wait for me.

Ava felt her cheeks get hot and looked up to find Jackson smiling at her, fully dressed in jeans and a plain white t-shirt that was a little tight across his broad chest and shoulders. His eyes settled comfortably right where the robe she wore didn't quite close. She was suddenly very, very aware that she was only wearing a robe, and that she was supposed to be wearing even less.

"Is this for real?" she asked, holding up the note.

"Completely." He came towards her, and her heart sped up perceptibly, but he only put his packages on the countertop: one red envelope and one pastry box. He leaned against the counter next to her and said, "And now you've disobeyed an order."

Disobeyed. She couldn't help but remember that he'd referred to "discipline" earlier.

"Not on purpose," she said, inexplicably nervous. "Besides, what were you going to do, surprise me with baked goods while naked?"

Desperate for a distraction, she flipped open the lid of the box to reveal her favorite: red velvet cupcakes with buttercream icing. She'd tried to make them for him once, ages ago. He remembered. Now her heart stopped altogether.

"Not exactly," he drawled, and took her hand in his as he pushed off the counter, pulling her around to face him. The robe came loose and opened an inch. She was naked underneath, just barely dry after her shower.

Well, not dry anymore.

He pressed her hand to the counter, rendering her immobile, and flicked the robe open.

"That's better," he said. His gaze took in her body from her toes up to her face. She could see the primal desire in his stare, in the twitch of his jaw, even in the way he breathed. *This must be what it's like to be hunted.*

Except prey probably didn't feel this good when it was caught.

"No cupcakes, then?" she said, her voice small.

"That depends," he said, "on whether you're a quick learner."

"What do I have to learn?"

"Submission."

Ava swallowed. This was it—this was what she'd signed up for. She could do this, this carnal, primal thing. He let her hand go, boxing her in against the counter with his body, and tilted her face up toward his, his thumb brushing softly against her lower lip. Oh God, yes, she could do this.

"What does that mean?" she asked.

"It means I'm going to teach you."

"You are," she said. It wasn't a question. She knew it already. She already wanted him again, more than was healthy, more than she could handle while still being able to think rationally.

"That was the deal, *Frida*. I'm going to teach you to submit," he said, stripping off her robe. "Starting with the physical."

chapter 8

Ava stood naked before him, shaking. She didn't know what to do. Was she supposed to respond a special way? Was there —

"Shh," he said. He knew what she was thinking. He ran his fingers lightly over her shoulders.

"Do you want me — ?"

"Quiet, Ava," he said, his voice so low it was almost a growl. "It's all I can do not to make love to you right here."

She opened her mouth, then closed it again. That didn't sound all that bad.

"But that wouldn't help you much," he continued. He breathed in through his nose and sighed. Then his grey eyes sparkled, and he grinned. "I'll tell you what I'm gonna do: I'm gonna make a little concession to myself. You know how you have a safeword?"

Ava nodded. If he thought she could speak like

an intelligent adult while his thumb circled around her nipple like that, he was insane.

"Well, I'm gonna give myself an access word."

She slowly came back into focus. She managed to say, "What's that?"

"Exactly what it sounds like, Ava. You hear it, you get down on all fours, and—"

"Give you…access." She bit her lip to keep from smiling, even though she felt nervous as all hell. That was just... He didn't need to know how much that excited her.

He smiled, like he knew anyway. He probably did.

"That's right," he said, and let his hand fall down the front of her body until it rested on her mons. Just…resting there. Tormenting her. "You hear me say…'red velvet,' and you do just that."

Red velvet. Of course. She was starting to breathe fast.

"What if I'm not naked?"

"You *get* naked," he said. "At least where it counts."

Oh God.

He dipped his fingers between her legs, as though he were just checking to see if she were wet. She knew she was. He gave her a smug grin; now he knew, too.

Then he stepped back from her, his sudden absence making her feel almost cold in the well-heated apartment, looked her up and down again, and regretfully said, "All right, robe back on. I can't stand it. And we've got a game to play."

He walked into the living room while Ava frowned and gathered the robe about her. She was more confused than ever now, but two things she was sure of: she was no longer naked, and Jackson Reed was no longer touching her. Both of those things seemed like steps backward, especially if the alternative was talking.

She followed him to find that he was seated on his couch in front of the giant window that looked north and west over the city and the Hudson River. There were quite a few other luxury high-rises in the West Village now, enough that she was sure some of the neighbors could see in. Jackson didn't seem to care. He had a yellow legal pad and a pen.

"I was gonna come in and make you come about a dozen times before we got to this," he said, pointing at the legal pad. "But then you were disobedient."

Ava groaned. She tried not to think about what "disobedient" implied.

She asked, "What is this, an interview?"

Ava hated interviews. She always had, even back in school. Especially back in school, when companies were recruiting from the graduating class. Most of her life had involved putting on a front, but somehow the interview setting just shined a spotlight on all the pretense, which made her feel like a total fake.

"Kinda. Stand there." He pointed a few feet in front of him, right in front of the window.

"You know I hate interviews."

"I know *why* you hated most interviews. I'm guessing it's still for the same reason."

She fumbled with her robe, cinching it tighter about her waist. That window was making her nervous. She thought she could see the shadows of inhabitants in other buildings, moving about in their own lives. Could they see her?

You're just nervous in general, Ava. Calm down.

Jackson snapped his fingers, bringing her attention back to him. He had on a serious face, but she could tell there was a smile underneath it. He was enjoying this on several levels.

"You didn't have time to snoop around very much, did you?" he said.

Ava blushed. "I didn't *snoop*."

"You see the chest over there?"

Ava had thought it was an end table, next to a chair positioned across from the sofa where Jackson sat. He was actually reclined quite comfortably, his white t-shirt stretched across his torso and his arms spread over the back of the couch. She tried to give him an irritated look, but even his arrogance was sexy. Infuriating.

"Now I do, yes," she answered.

"Drag it over to where you are now."

Ava almost made some smart remark, but thought better of it. This was what she had agreed to. "Yes, sir," she said, though she couldn't keep the sarcasm out of her voice completely.

"Careful, Ava."

The chest wasn't as heavy as it looked, but it was large and awkward, and it was nestled between that chair and a lamp, right up against the wall. There wasn't a good place to grab hold of it. She struggled a bit, maneuvering it out to a place where she could grasp both sides. As she dragged it backwards into the center of the room, she stepped on the oversized robe, pulling it loose. It fell down over one shoulder, and she looked at the giant window again, and the view of New York. She moved to cover herself.

"Leave it alone," Jackson said sharply.

Surprised, she turned back around to face him. His tone had changed again. She'd obeyed unquestioningly, automatically.

Jackson still leaned back on his expensive looking black sofa, relaxed but alert, his athletic body seeming to revel in the sheer physicality of being. But his eyes were gleaming. Attentive. Ava hugged what remained of the robe to her, already feeling naked.

"Open the chest," he said.

Ava did. She couldn't help but look inside, and, for a moment, she held her breath. It was a treasure trove of things she'd only seen online or read about in books. Ropes, harnesses, vibrators (she had greater familiarity with some of those), handcuffs, all sorts of leather things, a black bar. They all passed by in a blur of potential. She felt slightly dizzy, and her heart beat uncomfortably in her chest. She couldn't tell if she was excited or afraid.

"Ava, pay attention." She looked back to Jackson. The chest's contents made her feel inexperienced and unprepared, aroused and apprehensive. She was glad not to have to look at it anymore.

"I have two sets of questions for you. To the first, you will answer yes or no," he said, and she glanced at the legal pad. "But you will answer without knowing what the questions are."

She looked at him. "What?"

"Exactly what I said. First, reach into the chest and pull out the first thing you touch. Don't look.

67

Do it blind."

Ava turned toward the chest without thinking, her hand reaching down.

"I said: don't look."

His voice cracked the suddenly still air, and again, without thinking, she looked away. It was ridiculous, this automatic obedience. And where just a few moments ago she'd been relieved to push the chest and its contents out of her mind, now all she could think about was what was inside. It was very awkward to try to reach into the chest without looking; she had to sort of bend sideways, keeping her eyes averted. The robe slipped further, and she remembered not to touch it. Her breast would be visible now.

Her fingers felt something round, and she clasped it. *Must be the black bar*. Safe enough, she supposed. She didn't really know. She lifted it out of the chest and looked to Jackson.

"Stop there. Now answer: yes or no?"

She still didn't understand. Ava wasn't someone to do things she didn't fully understand. How could you plan, how could you decide how to present yourself if you didn't know what you were doing?

"Answer me, Ava. Quickly."

"Yes."

That surprised her. She'd said yes, blindly. Jackson smiled. He looked satisfied. His eyes flashed, and he leaned forward.

"Good. Look at it. Do you know what it is?"

It was the black bar, obviously. She hefted it and shook her head.

"It's called a spreader bar."

Ava felt her whole body stiffen. A spreader bar. It was probably exactly what it sounded like. She looked at it more closely and saw attachments, cuffs. A dull beat had started somewhere deep inside her, something she felt right behind her clit. She licked her lips and looked at Jackson. He was grinning again, that same damn grin.

"Look at you, catching on," he said. "Or so you think. You know what, we'll switch the order up. Give me another answer."

"No." He raised an eyebrow, and she quickly said, "I mean, that's my next answer. No."

Now he laughed at her. "Just out of spite, huh? Thing is, Ava," he said, leaning even farther forward, his hands coming together in front of him like he was making a very grave promise, "you might regret that."

She didn't have time to figure out what that meant. The next set of questions went quickly. She got tired of guessing what his game was, of trying to figure out what she was saying yes or no to, and the more fatigued she got, the more she said yes. She never would have predicted that, but Jackson didn't seem surprised. And by the end, she had a pile of toys—or pieces of equipment, or whatever they were—in front of her, each and every one representing a kind of promise. If she looked at any one of them for too long, she got nervous, and scared. That's when she looked back at Jackson.

She was even wetter than before.

"Now," he said, "do you want to know what the questions were?"

She looked nervously at the riding crop. "Of course I do. But I can guess," she said too quickly.

That impulse felt familiar, the impulse to be right. To be ahead of the curve. To be in control.

"You can guess," he said smoothly, "but you'll be wrong."

Ava couldn't stop herself from piping up again, even though she knew she was pushing her luck. "It was about what...things we'll use," she said, gesturing at the pile in front of her.

"Sort of. I just had you take that stuff out to mess with you," he said, smiling, "and because I got to watch your face while you did it."

She was only half kidding when she said, "You bastard."

He rose, lightning quick, and pulled at the tie that held her robe closed. All the lights were on in the apartment, and it had started to get dark outside. The huge window loomed over Ava, reminding her that she'd soon be completely visible.

"I will spank you, Ava," he said. He was very calm. "And I'll do it right in front of the window."

She honestly couldn't tell if she wanted that or dreaded it. What had he already done to her?

"I'm sorry," she said.

"Take off the robe."

She hesitated and he did it for her — the third time in less than a day that he'd stripped her — leaving her naked in the well-lit living room in front of the huge window. He bunched the robe his hands and threw it back at the sofa, well beyond her reach. And then he just stood near her, not touching her, looking down at her as she held her hands up to her chest, trying to cover herself somehow in front of that big window.

"Will you tell me what they were?" she asked, her eyes cast downward. She couldn't stand it.

"They were about what I'm going to do to you."

She felt something in her belly flutter. "When?"

"When I feel like it. Soon. Maybe now."

"But I don't know what I agreed to," she said, hugging her arms to her chest.

"That's right," he said, reaching up to push a tendril of hair behind her ear. "Of course, you don't need to know. You're mine, remember?"

That phrase, "you're mine," felt like something strong, something she could grab hold of to help her stand up when she was feeling so weak. He hadn't touched her in what seemed like forever, but she was still feeling overwhelmed. He always had her number. He was always the only one who could see through her crap, and apparently he still could. Ava realized that he'd wanted her exhausted, mentally, too strung out to fight him, or herself.

"Smart man," she whispered.

He pretended not to hear her. Instead, he kissed her, quick and hard, crushing her naked body into his. Then he let her go.

"Cuff yourself," he said, gesturing at the handcuffs on the floor. He walked past her. She could hear him messing with something behind her even as she bent down to retrieve the cuffs.

"If you want to know the questions you've already answered," he said from somewhere behind her, "you'll answer a few more. This time, real questions, real answers. Otherwise, you'll just get a bunch of surprises."

Apparently he remembered how she hated

surprises, too. *Smart, smart man.*

Ava stared at the handcuffs, glinting silver in the light from the overhead, wondering at what they meant to her. A week ago she might have fantasized about this, but only in a strictly theoretical sense. She never would have allowed herself to be in a position to be confronted with the actual, real life possibility of being handcuffed by a man who was about to fuck her. If asked, she would have said maybe, one day, but it was a big step.

That step didn't seem so big now, up close. Or maybe it was Jackson who made it feel normal, less terrifying. It just seemed…inevitable.

Stop thinking, Ava.

She cuffed herself and turned to show him.

He looked down at her cuffed wrists and attached a length of soft black rope with a clip on the end to the cuffs with a definite *clink*. The rope extended to the other side of the room, where it was attached to a pulley that he'd hung on an eyehook that protruded from the wall. She jerked at the rope and the pulley gave slightly. There was some slack on the line. She followed it, and saw that Jackson held the other end in his hand.

He looked at her right back. Then he looked at her hands, cuffed, but still held up so they covered her breasts. His eyes flickered to the window and back to her.

"Close the chest and sit on it," he said, and returned to his seat on the sofa opposite her.

Bewildered, Ava did as he said. Part of her felt like this was ridiculous. She was naked and restrained in plain view of much of Manhattan.

And he hadn't touched her since he'd come back. She'd been aching for him for hours now, and the more she thought about it, the more the pressure behind her clit grew. It was making it hard to focus, hard to think.

She remembered what he'd said only that morning, when she'd tried to run out: *You've been thinking for ten years. How's that worked out for you?*

She looked at the grey eyed man who sat across from her, his face giving nothing away. Could he really know her that well? Still, after all this time?

"Spread your legs for me," he said, and began to slowly gather the slack on the line.

Ava looked out on the city and up at the windows of other apartments.

"Jackson, the window..."

"Don't make me repeat myself."

Ava took a deep breath and scooted up to the edge of the chest, the metal studs along its edges digging into her soft skin. She risked another quick look to the window. She wished she hadn't; it was dark outside now, and there were lights on in other apartments. She must be completely visible to anyone who cared to look. She brought her cuffed hands to her chin, hiding her breasts, and gingerly began to spread her legs.

"Wider, Ava," Jackson said, frowning. "Don't mess around."

Why was this so difficult? To just spread bare, like that. Even in front of Jackson. Perhaps especially in front of Jackson.

Slowly she inched her legs apart, balancing on her toes, until her legs could get no wider. She'd always been flexible. Her chest fluttered nervously as she hugged her breasts with her arms, her hands still cuffed together, until she looked up and saw Jackson's face, raw and hungry and utterly uncomposed for the first time since they'd been reunited. He was staring at her with his mouth slightly open. For a moment, she thought he might jump up right then and...

"Very nice," he said hoarsely.

She smiled.

"First question," he said, rising from his seat and walking towards her. "What is your favorite sexual fantasy?"

Ava blinked. She had a lot of fantasies. One by one, they flashed across her mind, but she didn't focus on the sex, or the situations, or those key moments that made any fantasy a...fantasy. For the first time, Ava realized that the one thing they all had in common was the kind of man—or *the* man—who starred in the leading role.

It was shattering.

Had she really been thinking about him all these years? Had it really been always, only, forever him? What the hell was she doing here, thinking she could get away with just sex, that this wouldn't...

"Ava."

He was standing over her now, looking down. He wrapped the length of black rope around one of his hands and began to pull.

"Stay where you are, keep your legs spread, and *answer me.*"

She saw the coils of rope begin to pile up, and she felt the tug on her wrists. Slowly, the rope began to pull her wrists up and back, towards the ceiling behind her, forcing her to uncover her breasts. He kept going until her arms were held up above her head, bent at the elbows. She was totally bare now. Physically.

"Ava…"

"This," she said softly. "Being tied down. Captured. Taken."

By you.

Jackson locked the rope and knelt down beside her. He reached for the spreader bar at her feet, then stopped, his gaze falling on her spread sex. He placed one large hand on her knee and slowly pushed up the length of her leg, his thumb pressing into her thigh, until he couldn't stand it anymore and he bent down to kiss her between the legs. Ava felt his lips surround her clit, and his hot tongue worked on her until she uttered a low, begging moan.

She cried out in protest when he pulled away. He turned back to the spreader bar, as though he hadn't just sent her sky high only to leave her there without release. Her legs were shaking as he fastened the cuffs to her ankles. She couldn't close her legs now if she wanted to.

"You're lucky, Ava," he said, resting his hands on her hips as he looked at her face. "You remember that first question, the one you answered 'yes' to so bravely?"

She nodded, trying not to breathe too hard.

"The question was whether or not you'd be allowed to come."

"Oh, please," she begged.

He laughed.

"Next question," he said, and selected a large,

textured, blue vibrator. "I want to know more about these fantasies. What do you think about? What gets you off?"

She shook her head, afraid to speak. She wasn't trying to be disobedient; she just didn't want to tell him the whole truth. He'd be gone in a week. He'd said no strings. How would he react if she said, "You?"

Jackson frowned and grabbed the riding crop. Quickly, he swatted both of her nipples—one, two. The sudden, sharp sting took her breath away and set the rest of her on fire.

"Tell me. Don't think. Answer."

"Being powerless. Being..." She gasped as she felt the pull on the rope again, and she had no choice but to lean back. Her abdominal muscles burned, and her hips strained until she was lying prone on her back, her arms pulled back behind her, immoveable, her breasts falling slightly to the side, her legs held apart by the spreader bar. She couldn't see him now, couldn't see where he was, or what he was about to do.

"Being under your control," she finished. She was panting.

"Good," he said from somewhere in front of her spread legs. "You answered 'no' to anal, though I'm considering a veto on that, I've got to tell you."

She clenched involuntarily. He laughed. *Oh God, he could* see *that.*

"I'm not done with these questions, Ava. You've got to relax."

And she felt his finger slip inside her, quickly, as though just testing. She didn't even have time to miss it before it was replaced with the head of something larger — much larger. Something cool and rubbery.

The vibrator.

She tried to think. It had been big, as big as Jackson himself. God, she wished he would just…

She cried out as he pushed it inside her. Not knowing it was coming made it seem about five times as big, and he filled her to the hilt. He moved it around inside her, pivoting in a slow circle. Her hips tilted up as far as they would go, and her back arched.

"Goddamn, that's beautiful," she heard him say.

She didn't think she could speak.

"C'mon, stay with me," he said, and came around her side, one hand still holding the vibrator inside her, the other smoothing the hair on her head. She felt like she was stretched tight and thin, impossibly so, like a bubble that was about to burst, and she had no idea what would happen when she did.

"Ava, look at me," he said, and his free hand moved to her breasts. She did, and she realized her lips were pressed tight together, like there was something she was trying hard not to say.

He pulled the vibe out, slowly, and pushed it back in. She groaned.

"You get off on being under my control?" he said. She nodded.

He fucked her a little faster with the vibe.

"On being vulnerable?" he asked.

Again, she nodded. She felt tears welling up in her eyes. She had no idea why she would be crying.

"On being with me?" he said.

Oh God, please… `She didn't want it to be true.

Why would he ask her that, why would he...

She writhed, and he held the back of her head and looked into her eyes.

"Why did you run away from me?" he said.

She shook her head and tears fell out of her eyes. She was crying. She couldn't do this. She could do just sex, she couldn't do...

"Please," she begged.

His eyes softened, and his thumb brushed her cheek before he kissed her. "Shhh," he said. "You don't have to answer, it's ok."

Then he turned the vibe on and fucked her with it until she came, screaming his name.

chapter 9

Jackson had been rocked by Ava's orgasm almost as hard as she had—he was sure of it. Just the sight of her, flushed, a sheen of sweat shining across her arched body as she was pushed over the edge— Jackson was no choir boy, he'd seen plenty of women enjoy themselves, but that was the most beautiful thing he had ever seen. If he could make that happen every day, he'd be happy.

But it had come with a price, for both of them. He'd done it again. He'd pushed her too far, too fast, and only just caught himself in time. He'd felt the old self-loathing rising within him as he had uncuffed her and carried her to the couch, and it had kept him from being fully in the moment with her. Now, as he held her close, wrapped in his old bathrobe, and he rubbed her legs up and down to keep them from cramping, he didn't want to be thinking about anything else. He wanted to be there, with her, only.

Too bad.

He had to think about things he'd rather not, or risk hurting her. Risk becoming the person he'd fought so hard not to be.

Fine.

His original plan—if it could be called that—was still a good one. He knew he knew Ava better than he'd known anyone—really, better than he supposed he had a right to, after ten years. He just did. Couldn't explain it. Knew enough to know that he had to tread carefully, that there was something deep inside her that she had to learn to let go of slowly, and he knew that for an over-thinker like Ava, the way to do that was through the physical. Just side step the rational altogether, let her body show her the way forward, and her mind might choose to follow. Otherwise, she'd fight. He could see it happening a little already. He'd seen her do it over a million little things back in school.

Ava was a fighter in every possible way. He figured she had reasons to be.

She was starting to come to, her heart slowing, her breathing returning to normal. She curled into his chest more, and he squeezed her tight. He wouldn't let her go until he had to.

He let his face fall, his lips brushing her head. He'd been careful, hadn't he? All that work he'd done, all that introspection, all those years learning about how to be a loving dominant. Hell, he'd read books. That had worked, hadn't it? He hadn't ended up that way. He'd never wanted to hurt anybody; he'd only been thinking about her welfare, how she felt, what she needed.

And yet, still, he'd pushed her too far. Pushed her past a boundary that mattered to her.

If he had hurt her—again—he'd never forgive himself.

"Hey," she said, and looked up at him with those sleepy blue eyes.

"There you are," he said, and kissed her forehead. "How're you doing?"

She seemed to know what he was asking. It was in the pause, in her slow blink, in her thoughtful expression. Like she was taking the time to compose herself, make a decision. She must have been coming to in his arms for a while. That, or he was so crazed that he was imagining things.

Finally, she gave a lazy, playful shrug. "I guess I've been worse."

He laughed out loud with relief. She might still be coming out of subspace, but he knew Ava. And she wouldn't have forgotten the questions he'd asked. Maybe she wasn't answering them, but at least she wasn't holding it against him.

"Oh, really?"

She squealed as he went in to tickle the bottoms of her feet and rolled off of his lap with surprising agility, considering. She hopped away, robe wrapped snugly around her, shaking her finger at him before he could get up.

Jackson stared after her. With just her expression, just that gesture, it was like she'd sent them back in time. Just like it had been when they'd last stayed up all night, talking and laughing, as though he hadn't lost ten years with her. Like they were still young and stupid, and free to joke around without worrying about what unseen landmines lay beneath the surface, what emotional baggage lay around, just waiting to trip them up. He knew it couldn't last like that, that the past would have to be dealt with. But at that moment, he chose to believe it would last at least a little bit longer.

"Where do you think you're going?" he asked as she sauntered towards the kitchen counter.

"For some inexplicable reason, I'm feeling kind of hungry," she said over her shoulder. "And I distinctly remember cupcakes."

She flipped open the box, then paused as something else caught her attention. She held up the red envelope he'd brought back with him and shot him a questioning look.

"What's this?"

"You'll find out."

She smiled sweetly, bringing her cupcake back into the living room where she sat on his toy chest—he assumed so she could taunt him while she licked icing off of her fingers. "Tell me now," she said. "And you can have some of this."

Jackson hadn't pulled every string imaginable to score the most exclusive invitation in all of New York City—hell, the entire east coast, maybe—just to blow the surprise over a cupcake. A cupcake that he had bought. He told her as much.

"Unless you were talking about something else," he said, standing up. He was still hard from making her come, and he hadn't forgotten what she had looked like, spread and prone. "But I thought I should give you a break. I put you through quite a workout."

"Speak for yourself," she said, smiling. She

licked the last of the icing from her fingertips. "I've stayed in shape."

He couldn't deny that.

"What would you do," she said airily, waving the envelope at him, "if I just opened it?"

She was playing at being a brat, but that would be bad. Ava's impish streak aside, the invitation needed to be presented sealed, or they wouldn't get in. He'd had to go all the way to midtown in the snow to pick it up in person. He glowered at her.

"Ava, don't try it."

"Or what?"

"You've got quite an attitude for a sub, you know that?"

"I'm not all that submissive outside the bedroom, Jacks," she said.

And she smiled that charming smile at him again, the one that let him know she thought she had him in the palm of her hand. Well, she did — it was true. But he had a hold on her, too.

"Red velvet," he said.

Her eyes got really wide, really fast. He watched her memory go into overdrive, watched her remember exactly what those two words meant.

"I know you're anything but submissive outside the bedroom, Ava, and believe me when I say that I love that about you," he said as he walked toward her. "But this week, sweetheart, the whole damn world is the bedroom."

He wanted to smile, remembering how excited she'd gotten when he had given her an access word, and seeing the flush creeping up her neck now. But he kept his face stern. He stood over her while she looked up at him with those big eyes, and began to unbuckle his jeans.

"Red velvet," he said again, and this time he put that Dom edge in his voice.

She blinked once, twice. Then she slowly took off the robe, got on her knees, and bent over the chest.

He'd only been half-serious, but looking at her smooth skin, her soft thighs, and the pink of her lips quivering there, just waiting for him, he couldn't resist. He freed his engorged cock as soon as he could, grabbed hold of her shoulder with one hand, spread her with the other, and mounted her.

He plunged into her, wanting to feel himself buried to the hilt inside her. He heard her cry out and she bucked backward, her head dipping low as she drove her hips to meet him. Holy fuck, there was no one like her — there never had been anyone like her. She fit him to perfection. He fell on top of her, wrapping his hand in her hair and pulling her up so he could play with her breasts while he rode her.

He fucked her long and hard, holding off while she came twice around his tortured cock, until he couldn't stand it anymore. He felt his mind floating away, and all that was left was the pure animal need, and he grabbed hold of her hips and drove into her until he lost himself in her. This time, it was Jackson screaming her name.

He collapsed on top of her, and they stayed like that for some time, the red envelope lying on the floor in front of them like a promise.

chapter 10

I am such a dumbass.

Ava caught herself picking at the loose threads on the edges of her peacoat, balled her hand into a fist, and smiled nervously at Jackson. They were bundled together in the backseat of an expansive, comfortable town car, speeding towards some secret destination, to do Ava had no idea what. She was both excited and petrified, which was becoming the standard combination around Jackson.

Somehow he'd already gotten to her. In just over twenty-four hours, he'd already gotten closer to her by showing her how much he understood— without words—what she wanted, what she *needed*, physically and emotionally, more than anyone else ever had. That sinking feeling in the pit of Ava's stomach was telling her that she'd have to build her walls back up, and she'd have to do it quickly, if she were going to survive this week with her heart intact.

Her feelings of anxiety had started small after that first twenty-four hours. They had been a glorious twenty-four hours, Ava had to admit. She'd be thinking about the things he'd done to her until the day she died. And all the sex hadn't left her much time or energy for worrying about each and every little thing. The result had been so deceptively easy, as though nothing had changed. Feeling close to him had just snuck up on her, as though they'd just picked up where they'd left off, like they'd never hurt each other, like ten years hadn't passed them by.

But, Ava thought ruefully, *they have.*

That's what had started small, she realized: the reminders that it really had been ten years. That they both really had lived lives in that time, and things were different now. That there were so many things she didn't know about him, so many things he didn't choose to share with her. It made her realize that he'd never shared much with her.

Take, for example, the fact that Jackson was obviously both rich and powerful now. Not that those things didn't suit him—in fact, now Ava would have had trouble imagining him any other way—but he no longer felt like a peer. That morning, he had made an important phone call and talked about possible stock options and underwriting from big banks and when to leak what news to which tech magazines, and she felt totally lost. What world did he live in now? It didn't feel like a world she could possibly understand.

And that had just been this morning. He'd made that call while she lay next to him, naked.

Then there was his manner. It was...different. More authoritative then she remembered, more in control. He was still him, but somehow more so. She didn't know what to make of it, exactly, but she knew she had no idea where it had come from.

And that made her afraid. Because this was a temporary arrangement, and she was already in serious danger of getting lost in what was essentially a vacation to the past, the past as it should have been, and not something that could reasonably be expected to survive into the future.

By the time they'd gotten into the car, that red envelope secured away in Jackson's pocket, Ava was actively looking for more telltale differences, more indications of the distance between them. It was like she was hoarding them, clutching them to her like passing pieces of driftwood that might keep her from drowning in the way she felt about Jackson Reed.

This is not real life, Ava reminded herself for about the billionth time. *Eventually it will have to end. Keep it physical.*

"You ok?" Jackson asked, jolting her out of her head. He reached over and grabbed her hand. Just his touch electrified her all over again.

"Yeah," she lied. "Just wondering where you're taking me."

He smiled devilishly. It was hard not to smile back and mean it.

"You are going to love it," he said. "Almost as much as I'm going to love you loving it."

And he waggled his eyebrows at her. She

couldn't help but laugh out loud. "You are ridiculous," she said.

"You have no idea, sweetheart."

He pulled her across the seat and nestled her in the crook of his arm. Ava leaned into him with a sigh and watched the snow-covered trees pass by. She tried hard to enjoy the moment and not think too much about the future while they sped through New York towards the unknown.

~ ~ ~

Ava managed to calm herself during the long drive, but then became unaccountably nervous again as their car pulled into a long, wooded drive. Well, maybe not unaccountably. There was an insane fence—no, not a fence, a genuine stone *wall*—and then one of those imposing wrought iron gates that opened remotely when their car approached. They'd been driving on what was apparently private property for way too long. This obviously wasn't a normal house or building or whatever: it was an estate.

Ava wasn't wrong. They came around a bend in the gravel drive, and there was a stately, snow-covered gothic mansion, like something that had been lifted out of the English countryside and plopped down in the middle of this New York suburb.

"Where *are* we?" she asked.

"Bedford," Jackson answered. Bedford was a town a little north of the city. She punched his arm.

"You know that's not what I meant."

Jackson turned and gave her a serious look. "Narnia," he said.

"You're not going to tell me, are you?"

"I'm going to show you."

Ava reddened. What did *that* mean?

She only had time to think of a few possibilities, each more explicit than the last, before the car crunched to a slow stop in front of a grand, arched entrance. Ever the gentleman, Jackson helped her out of the car while the driver unloaded their bags. That was another thing she'd missed: Jackson's Oklahoma upbringing had done him right in some ways, even if he had always been reluctant to actually talk about it. Chivalry was not dead. Still, she looked at the luggage with a vague degree of discomfort. She didn't even know what they held. Jackson had called Bergdorff's and given them an amazingly accurate estimation of her measurements and told them to make up a bag. Ava hadn't known you could just...do that. She'd tried not to think about how many other women Jackson had done that for.

Jackson thumped on the trunk of the car, and they watched it drive off. As soon as it had rounded a curve, he wrapped his arms around her and kissed her.

"Was that a clue?" she asked, trying to regain her composure. The air between them was just cold and wet enough for their breath to hang in the air. Jackson's cheeks had started to get red already, and his grey eyes sparkled.

"Nah, that was just because I felt like it," he said, stooping to pick up the bags. "You hungry?"

Actually, she was starving. They'd barely had

time for breakfast in between all their extracurricular activities, and it was almost lunchtime. "Yes, now that you mention it, I'm kind of famished."

"Well, we'll go in and get some lunch first."

He walked toward the doors, blithely unaware that she stayed put. This annoyed her to no end.

"Jackson Reed, tell me where we are!"

Jackson looked over his shoulder, grinning broadly. "We're at Volare's Christmas retreat, sweetheart. Now get your ass in here before I feel the need to take measures."

A thrill passed through Ava's entire body. Volare's Christmas retreat? A BDSM *Christmas retreat?*

What the hell was that?

~ ~ ~

The place was just as immense and intimidating as it appeared from the outside. The ceilings in the entry hall were at least two stories high, maybe higher, and arched, like the inside of an ancient cathedral. There were so many nooks and crannies hidden away in shadow that the only possible intent was melodrama.

Jackson looked up and laughed softly.

"Bet Casper's up there," he said.

Ava felt her own laughter bubble up uncontrollably. "Are we in a gothic novel? Like, do you have a crazy wife up in the attic that I don't know about, and the housekeeper will try to make me go crazy?"

"Who told you about my wife?" Jackson deadpanned.

Ava laughed, but she already regretted the joke. How could she possibly feel insecure? She had no claim. It shouldn't bother her to think about Jackson's past or the women he'd known. Or knew. That was, in fact, a terrible sign that she wasn't doing such a hot job keeping those strings from just attaching themselves all over the place.

Smooth move, Ava. You don't need a meddling housekeeper to make yourself crazy, do you?

Ava shook her head and looked up to find Jackson studying her. He was about to say something when they were interrupted by a slim young man dressed in a tailored black suit. He had the longest eyelashes Ava had ever seen on a man.

Jackson handed him the red envelope.

"Thank you, Mr. Reed," the young man said, pocketing the envelope and gathering up their bags. "Master Roman is expecting you, but he's out until tomorrow evening. I'll take these up to your room."

"We'll have lunch first," Jackson said firmly, eyeing Ava. "Is it the room I had last time?"

Ava tried not to show her dismay. *Last time*. Of course he'd been there before. Odds were that he hadn't been alone. *Get over it, Barnett, this is exactly what you're not supposed to do!*

"Yes, sir."

"Then I know where it is. Can you take our coats?"

Ava didn't see how, but the young porter found a way to balance all their things on his thin frame. Jackson seemed to admire the effort the guy put into it. After some back and forth with Jackson retrieving things from his coat pockets and tipping the poor kid—who looked like he was about to tip over himself—they were off to lunch.

"I feel underdressed," Ava said. She was whispering in deference to the vaulted cathedral ceilings.

"Really? I was just thinking you were overdressed."

And just in case she didn't get his meaning, Jackson reached down and gave her ass a good squeeze. Ava pressed her lips together to keep from smiling. Trust Jackson to chase away crazy thoughts with some inappropriate touching.

"Incorrigible," she muttered.

They had the large, exquisitely furnished dining room mostly to themselves. There was a very quiet but intense couple off in a corner, easy enough to forget. Everything around them was decorated in ivory: the tablecloths, the chairs, and even the wallpaper, which was lightly flecked with gold. They'd been there all of thirty seconds before a white-coated waiter appeared out of nowhere to serve them coffee.

"What is this place, seriously?" Ava asked Jackson as the waiter faded away. Obviously the place was staffed, but she could already see that the staff had an almost spooky habit of melting out of sight when not needed. She was starting to feel completely out of place, and her anxieties about, well, pretty much everything, were returning in full force.

"What, you've never been to a secret, isolated estate for wealthy sexual deviants?" Jackson was hunting around for something in his pockets and missed Ava's expression.

"We're not deviants," she said.

He looked up, surprised. Concerned. "Of course not. I was joking. Ava," he said, reaching across the table to grasp her chin. "I was joking."

"I know. I'm sorry, it's just..."

She had been thinking about the first time they'd slept together, all those years ago. He seemed to know it. He looked at her for another moment, a beat longer.

"What?" she said.

"Just thinking. We're here for a reason, you know. I've got plans for you," he added with that sly, dark smile.

Adrenaline shot through her, and she suddenly became very aware of her entire body. It unnerved her that she had no idea what he could be planning. It was exciting, and yet, it was another reminder of how much she didn't know about this newer, older Jackson Reed.

But then, Jackson reached into the pocket of the blazer he was wearing over an old vintage t-shirt and dumped a few single serving dairy creamers on the table. He'd obviously brought them with him. It was apparently still the only stuff he'd put in his coffee. With deliberate care, Jackson took one of the gleaming silver forks and poked several holes in the top of a creamer.

The sense of *déjà vu* smacked into Ava at full force, knocking her out of herself and shrinking the world around them until she felt they were alone together in this moment. She remembered a late night in college, when she'd called Jackson after a night of partying, and he'd met her at an all night diner where they sat in comfortable silence while he did exactly what he was doing now: poking holes in the foil lid of the creamer, then tipping it over his coffee and squeezing out little streams of cream so that it was "like a little cow." He'd explained that to her with his shy, boyish grin, and then he'd laughed and done it all over again. It was silly, and kind of gross, and it was just a little way to play and have fun in the world, and she loved that he still did that. That he'd kept that weird little quirk. She loved that he was still that guy, even if he was now a world-conquering Dom, too.

She laughed softly. "Moo," she said.

"You making fun of me?" he said, looking up from his coffee. "You making fun of my cows? Say what you want about me, but leave my cows out of it."

"I didn't say anything," she demurred. "I think that was Bessie complaining."

"Now I know you're making fun of my cows."

"Moooo."

He shook his head, like a reluctant disciplinarian. Suppressing a smile he said, "Reeedddd..."

"Jackson!" The access word was a fantastic idea, but not in public!

"Velv—"

"You wouldn't! Not here!" Ava leaned forward across the table and jerked her head towards the oblivious couple in the corner, as though that could emphasize her point, acutely aware that this action pressed her breasts together in the low-cut v-neck sweater that Jackson had provided for her. By the looks of it, he was very aware of her breasts, too.

"As a matter of fact, I would. And that," he said, motioning towards her cleavage, "is not helping your case."

Ava didn't know what to say. She felt frozen, trapped between arousal and horror at the very idea of...

"You seem to have mixed feelings about that idea," Jackson said, sipping his coffee. "Interesting."

Ava was sure she would have had the perfect witty retort, she was sure she would have exactly figured out what she wanted and how to handle Jackson, if they had not been interrupted in the very next moment.

By a woman. A very thin, very elegant looking brunette, maybe a few years older than Ava, with her hair pulled back in a severe but fashionable sort of asymmetric knot, and a long, graceful hand that she let rest on Jackson's shoulder.

"You can imagine how surprised I am to see you here," the woman said to Jackson. She didn't look at Ava.

Jackson put his coffee down slowly and turned to meet the woman's gaze.

"Probably not as surprised as I am to see you, Lillian," Jackson said. "How are things back at ArTech?"

The woman called Lillian smiled. "Check your email." And then Lillian reached out and ruffled Jackson's hair. Ava had never been more irritated by a gesture in her entire life. "I'll be here for the weekend; I've had it planned for ages. Maybe I'll see you around the estate."

Lillian finally looked at Ava with a cool, flinty smile for one silent beat. Then she walked over to the quiet couple in the corner.

Ava tried to keep her voice as normal as possible. "Who was that?" she asked.

You have no claim on him, Ava. No reason to be jealous of grown up mean girls in expensive designer tops and skinny black jeans. Jackson hasn't lied to you; he hasn't hurt you.

Ava instinctively bit a nail at the thought of Peter, the only other guy she'd been with who'd claimed to be a Dom, and who had cheated all over the place. Peter was the reason she'd transferred schools, and so he was indirectly responsible for her meeting Jackson, but otherwise Peter wasn't worth thinking about. Instead she focused on Jackson, who, to her dismay, looked pretty perturbed.

"That was Lillian," Jackson said. "My chief operations officer."

Ava gave him a moment to continue. He didn't.

Well, if you have no claim on each other, there's no reason for this to be awkward. There's no reason not to ask him. It would be more awkward not to ask, right?

"That's all she is?" Ava asked. Her voice came out high and thin.

Jackson frowned. "That's all she is now."

Ava felt slightly queasy. *So maybe there was a reason not to ask.* Clearly this Lillian woman had been here before, to Volare, to this Country Kinkmas Estate or whatever the hell it was, with Jackson. That was just about the worst thing Ava could envision at that moment. It did not help in the least that, on top of just generally hating the idea of Jackson and anyone together, this was a clear indication that she was failing spectacularly at keeping her heart out of it.

Jackson didn't seem particularly happy, either. Just moments ago, everything had been relaxed, happy, with the promise of more incredible sex, and now they were sitting here in awkward silence, each of them apparently unhappy with something.

He said no strings, Ava. Don't make it a thing.

"Fantastic," Ava muttered, and blushed when Jackson looked up. She was saved — if that was the right word — by a further interruption.

"Jackson, you have to meet the Sharzis," Lillian cried from across the room. She smiled like someone out of a catalog. Ava didn't trust anything about her.

"Ava, we can leave if you want."

"It sounds like it's business, though." It was true. As much as Ava felt instinctively bound to hate Lillian, she recognized that tone: professional smooth talk. Lillian probably didn't mean to be working, either, but Ava knew you couldn't always pick and choose when a business opportunity arose.

Like, say, at a freaking BDSM Christmas retreat.

Ava honestly didn't know if she should be quite as mortified as she felt as Lillian maneuvered the previously unobtrusive couple over to their table. On the one hand, holy crap, all of these people were now aware that she was at BDSM club. On the other hand, so were they. Nothing about this was comfortable. It was like everyone's private business was just everywhere.

Even so, the Sharzis proved to be a dignified

couple with gracious manners.

Oh God, don't think about what they're into!

Too late, Ava realized that she probably *looked* as surprised and uncomfortable as she felt, based on the quizzical looks she was getting.

Lillian smoothed it over.

"Jackson, the Sharzis are extremely interested in ArtLingua."

Jackson frowned. "We haven't announced that publicly yet," he said.

"That's part of what's so intriguing," said Mrs. Sharzi. She had the rare beauty of a woman in her late fifties, and she seemed comfortable in her skin in a way that Ava envied. "Formalizing a visual, artistic language, into a series of—what did you call them? Linguistic automata? Or, I suppose, a new language all itself. I'm not sure I understand it," she laughed, "but I can tell you we'd be interested in your next round of financing."

Language through art? Ava looked wonderingly at Jackson, not seeing him necessarily as he was, but him as he had been, years ago: a fellow student in her art classes, a brilliant computer programmer just learning about what one could do through artistic expression. Eager to learn with her, to have her teach him. He'd been like a little kid with a new toy back then.

"That's what your company does?" she asked.

"Not yet," Jackson said. His face was darkening by the second. "Right now it's just apps and social networking."

"He's being modest," Lillian assured the Sharzis. "He's a genius. The commercial problem solving applications alone—"

"That's not why I built it," Jackson said. "It could be critical for various behavioral therapies, and people with verbal difficulties." He shot Lillian a *look*. It was a look that said entire paragraphs, the kind of look that can only exist between people who have had a lot to say to each other at one time or another, and Ava wasn't sure exactly what it meant. For the first time, she felt very much on the outside looking in.

Lillian flashed that catalog smile at the Sharzis. "Well, all the best ideas are inspired by the desire to help people. Of course, we know we owe it to our investors—"

Jackson rose from the table and pointed at Ava. "Actually, I owe it all to her," he said. "And no one else."

Lillian paused for just one second. "Oh, are you an artist?" she said, finally looking directly at Ava.

Ava shook her head. "Not anymore," she said quickly. *That* was personal.

There was a polite silence.

"I'm sorry, but you'll have to excuse us," Jackson said, staring at Ava. "We just got here, and need to settle ourselves in."

He took Ava's hand. It wasn't a request. They were leaving.

Bewildered, Ava followed him out of the dining room, moving at a brisk trot to keep up with his long strides. For once she didn't care about what the people she'd just met thought of her, or if she'd made the desired impression, or about what the social undercurrents she'd perceived actually meant in context. Ava was thinking about only one thing.

What does Jackson Reed think he owes me?

chapter 11

Jackson seethed. The halls of the Bedford Volare estate had never seemed so long and serpentine before this, but then he'd never wanted to get away quite like this, either. He'd had to sit there and watch Ava close up when confronted with other people, with the business of his outside life, with Lillian. Perhaps most of all with Lillian. Ava had been open to him just barely, slowly, letting him in inch by inch, and then...

GodDAMN it.

He'd seen her reassemble her armor lightning quick, retreating into herself to watch and observe, the way she used to around people she didn't trust. Retreating away from him.

Ava was never one to be comfortable baring herself in public. He remembered the first time she'd shown him some of her private paintings, how different they'd been, how clear it had been to him that the things she did in the studio were deliberately for public consumption, and a poor representation of the beauty she was capable of.

He'd seen her face when Lillian had touched his shoulder, too. That hadn't been good. Too late, Jackson had remembered that the relationship Ava almost never talked about, the one that had hurt her so much that she had transferred in her senior year and cut herself off from her former life, had involved some kind of infidelity. Only he wasn't sure how, or who, or what. Christ, he wished he'd been smart enough or wise enough or just good enough to just *listen* when she'd tried to open up back then.

When he thought back on that time, Jackson always remembered, most of all, the sensation of moving forward. Both he and Ava had been characterized by a kind of relentless forward momentum, a need to leave the past behind without so much as a backwards glance. That was the thing that had drawn them together, besides their inherent affinity for each other.

The thing was, it seemed like Ava's forward momentum had tripped up since then. Like she'd made a wrong turn somewhere, or had gotten stuck in the wrong gear, or had stalled out. He was more and more certain now, the more time they spent together, that something just hadn't come together for her. And he had to face the fact that he, Jackson Reed, might be partially responsible for that.

Especially because Jackson had been all jammed up, too, ten years ago, and Ava Barnett had been the person to set him right. Even though she'd run away, Ava had left him with something real, something tangible, to guide him through the last ten years. That picture she'd painted for him had become without a doubt his most prized possession. Now it was hidden behind his shirts in the back of his closet, lest Ava see it and get kind of spooked. One day, he'd tell her what it meant to him. One day, he'd explain to her that she'd been his north star, and why. But in the meantime, he had to face the fact that she'd left him the thing that had saved him, and he'd left her with nothing but a bad memory and some emotional scars.

And she didn't even paint anymore.

That had hit Jackson like an actual punch to the gut. She didn't paint. He was probably the only person on the planet who knew what that meant. The way Ava had said it, it had seemed like even she didn't know what it meant, like it had been so long that she'd forgotten.

"Jackson!" she called from behind him, and he stopped and turned to see that she was actually panting a little, her chest heaving up and down in that low cut sweater. He'd practically run them through this big old house, just looking for a place where they could be alone together with no memories of anyone else. They were in an old hallway in one of the wings—some unused part of the house, judging by the faded wallpaper and the dust in the corners. Ava was looking at him funny.

"What is *wrong* with you?" she said, brushing her auburn hair out of her face. "What was that about?"

She really didn't seem think it was at all strange that she would announce that she didn't paint. It made the distance between them suddenly vast and imposing, and Jackson couldn't stand it.

"I need you," he said.

She looked up at him. "What?"

"Now," he said, and pushed her against the wall. She grunted a little when her back hit the wall, and her hair fell back in front of her face. He pushed it out of the way and kissed her, hard.

He did what he wanted. He reached up under the brand new sweater to feel her breasts, pushing it up over her chest and unhooking her bra from the front. Then she was out in the open, disheveled looking, and it made him instantly hard. He bent down to take a sweet nipple in his mouth, and let his hands rove over her body until he found the hem of her skirt. He pushed it up over her hips, not caring that they were out in a hallway, not caring about anything at all besides pushing aside her panties and getting inside her.

"Jackson—"

He didn't want to talk for once, didn't want any more words to remind him of all the time that had passed, of all the things that had happened to her that he would never know about. He only wanted to be close to her. He covered her mouth with his and pushed his finger inside her, curling it the way she liked. He felt her bear down, and she moaned. She was already so goddamn wet, it was incredible.

He couldn't wait another second. He ripped at the zipper on his pants while she threw her arms around him, resting her head on his shoulder.

"Oh God," she said, so softly he almost didn't hear it.

And then he was out, his cock so hard it pulsed. He reached down and scooped her up into the air, so light he didn't even need the wall, and held her just above him while she wrapped her legs around him.

She touched his face and he lowered her onto his cock, filling her until she closed her eyes and sighed.

Then he dug his fingers into her flesh, pinned her against the wall, and drove into her until she came convulsing around him, drawing out his orgasm with great, shuddering breaths.

~ ~ ~

It wasn't until after they'd eaten lunch and gone on a walk around the grounds that Jackson figured out what he needed to do.

They were walking down the stone steps that led to an old quarry that had been fashioned into a pond that froze over reliably in winter when Jackson realized he was looking over his shoulder for Lillian. That sucked. He didn't want to be thinking about anything or anyone but Ava, but here he was, worried that Lillian would show up and give Ava the wrong impression. Again. Frankly, he was worried about dealing with Lillian, and about what that meant for the launch, but Ava was his priority.

And he was concerned about her. He was troubled by what he'd learned already, that she didn't paint anymore, that she considered that a part of her past. And that she was so uncomfortable being "out" as submissive, even in a place where the whole damn point was that you could be yourself. It suggested that maybe the problem wasn't other people. Maybe Ava just wasn't all that comfortable being herself.

Jackson had to admit that wouldn't surprise him. Ava was still the most guarded person he'd ever met, still had that armor that she could put on in a flash. He'd been wondering if she'd told anyone in her life where she was, for real, and then she'd gotten that mystery phone call. All he'd heard was, "yeah, still on that junket," and he'd known she'd kept it secret. She probably hadn't told anyone about him at all.

Damn, it's been just a few days, Jackson. Give the girl room to breathe. Well, that was as it was. And he had told her no strings.

But that didn't mean it wouldn't be good for her to accept herself in public.

Jackson smiled as Ava trudged back toward him through the snow, looking happy to see him. He had a plan now.

He took Ava's hand and cocked his head toward the pond.

"Everyone will come out ice skating here tonight," he said. "They'll light it up with lanterns and stuff."

She nodded in appreciation, looking out at the beautiful, thick ice, almost completely surrounded by steep, sheeted walls of rough-hewn rock. It looked like something out of a fairytale.

"It's nice to be rich, huh?" she said.

"I haven't found many things I care to spend money on. Maybe just one," he finished, giving her a sly look. It was corny, but he was kind of proud of that line.

She looked airily back at him. "Single serving

dairy creamers?"

That deserved a pile of snow on top of the head. She squealed with laughter as she ran, and by the time he caught her and had gotten his proper, snowy revenge, he was already wondering how he could possibly wait until after dinner to have her again. To avoid the temptation, he lifted her over his shoulder and carried her back to the house. He had arrangements to make.

chapter 12

Ava edged closer to the fire, wine glass in hand, and brooded. Jackson was planning something. Ever since she'd taken that stupid call from Alain while they were out walking, Jackson had had that look in his eye. That mischievous look that said he took as much pleasure in teasing her with offhand comments and allusions as he would in whatever it was that he had planned for her.

That look, and the way it made her feel all warm and mushy about Jackson, was one reason for the wine. The other was the general goings on at Camp Kinkmas, as Ava had come to think of the Volare retreat. The wine was meant to relax her while Jackson went about his preparations, whatever they were, and she was left in one of the common great rooms with the other guests.

The other guests at the *BDSM Christmas retreat*. Ava was pretty sure she'd never get over the fact that such a thing existed. The other guests, who had apparently planned some themed activities. The other guests, who included Lillian and her date, a cheerful looking salt-and-pepper gentleman who mostly seemed happy to have a date at all.

Jackson had allowed her exactly one glass of wine while he was off making his "arrangements." He didn't want her impaired, he'd said. As Ava watched while people picked names out of a hat for Volare's version of Secret Santa—whatever that entailed—she wondered if a glass of eggnog would technically be cheating. She didn't often indulge, given her family history, but this seemed like an exception.

The irony was, she *wanted* to be able to join in and have fun, even if she didn't want to be anyone but Jackson's Secret Santa gift. She just couldn't. For some reason, this was one situation where she couldn't become her usual social persona, laughing and playing along and charming everyone. There was some sort of block. She envied the others, though, having their fun. Even Lillian.

Nope, do not think about that. Do not think about Jackson and Lillian...

Ava's phone buzzed again on the low table beside the couch she'd claimed as her own. It was probably Alain again. She thought she'd blown him off pretty effectively when he'd called earlier, with her breezy lie about a junket, but apparently she'd sounded like she was having too much fun. Alain had wanted to know where it was, and she was sure he was calling to figure out how to crash the party.

The weird thing was, Ava still wasn't all that concerned. Objectively, she reasoned, it was actually pretty freaking worrying. She'd put a lot into her advertising career, into outwardly making herself into the kind of person who succeeded in the advertising world. And Ava cared about being successful.

Or she had. Whatever had driven her ambition before, this week seemed to be on the fritz. Right here, right now, with Jackson, it all seemed so totally alien to her. Like it didn't just belong to some other life, but to some other person.

My God, a few days of incredible sex, and I'm cracking up.

Didn't they say great sex was supposed to be *good* for you? Was supposed to totally bliss you out and make you all zen and focused? Leave it to Ava to lose her mind, instead.

Because she was feeling pretty anxious right now. She should be totally relaxed, finally in a place where her sexual submissiveness wasn't something she had to feel weird about, finally with a man she trusted, with no strings, and instead of being at ease, she was a total stress case. She did feel relaxed and at peace and safe when it was just her and Jackson. But somehow, having to face these people and be reminded that there was a real world out there…

Maybe it was because she knew it would have to end. That she'd have to return to that real world.

Maybe.

Or maybe she was just nervous as hell about whatever it was that Jackson was doing that required an hour of preparation.

"Ok, this is ridiculous," Ava said to herself as she downed the rest of her wine. She was on an actual sex vacation; she could be a little more cheerful. Screw the anxiety, and screw what anyone else thought of her, and screw...

"Just screw everything," she muttered.

"You only get to screw me." Jackson had snuck up on her. He was standing just behind her, looking all rugged in his snow boots and cable knit sweater.

"I am actually one hundred percent ok with that," she said.

He flashed her a grin before putting on his stern Dom face.

"Get up," he ordered.

Ava shivered a little and stood up. She was glad to have Jackson back to herself, and glad to have something else to think about.

He looked her up and down, and seemed to be studying her clothing. Was it not appropriate somehow? This was a pretty casual place, and besides, she was wearing what he'd brought for her. Just some leggings and a belted sweater dress and boots—nothing fancy, but still kind of classy.

"Is this ok?" she asked, looking down.

"It's fine," Jackson said, and hooked his fingers into her belt. Ava bit her lip and stayed quiet. She was already feeling the heat between her legs. He continued, "I have everything else we need. Follow me."

He set off at a brisk pace and she trotted after him, not caring now about what she did or did not feel a part of, or whether she was anxious, or what it meant to show this part of herself to other people. She stole a glance at the rest of the small weekend group as they left. They all had ice skates slung over their shoulders, and Ava remembered what Jackson had said about the quarry—it probably would be beautiful to skate there at night.

But not nearly as gorgeous as the man who was leading her...somewhere.

Outside?

Jackson had led her to a side door and was holding up a giant white parka.

"Put this on."

The parka was definitely overkill. It was only just cold enough for the snow to stay pristine and for their breath to hang in the air under the porch lights. Ava looked around as he lead her outside to the stone patio, expecting some sort of ice castle picnic or something. Instead, there was a two-person snowmobile just off the path. More like a sled, really, laden down with packages.

"Are we delivering Volare Christmas cheer?" She smiled. "Handcuffs? Various unmentionables?"

He laughed in a way that said Ava wasn't in on the joke. "Kind of."

Ava inhaled deeply. She didn't know what that meant, but maybe that was best.

"Ok, but do you know how to drive that thing?" she asked.

He looked at her, momentarily offended, and swung a leg over the seat. "I'd never be reckless with your safety. Get on."

She believed him. In fact, that was the one thing she felt certain of, and she grabbed hold of it in her mind, grateful to have something that made sense. She was already starting to feel disoriented again, drunk on anticipation and novelty and the previously unknown parts of her that kept surfacing with each new thing Jackson did to her, and it was nice to have something familiar and comforting. She did trust him. She straddled the seat and hugged Jackson tightly.

"You ready?"

She nodded into his back, and they were off. He went slowly at first, circling around the back of the huge house, leaving distinctive tracks in the otherwise virgin snow. In just a few minutes, they were far enough from the house that they relied on the moonlight, the pale light shining steadily on the expanse of snow. Ava had no idea where they were going. He'd started off in the direction of the quarry pond they'd seen the day before, but then he'd turned, and they were traveling up the side of a long hill with no evidence of other human beings anywhere.

She hugged him a little tighter, and he sped up.

Soon they were cresting the top of the hill, and Jackson slowed down as the coniferous pines started to get a bit thicker on the ground. By the time he brought them to a stop, Ava felt lulled into a kind of dream state. Everything around her was so beautiful, so peaceful. There was only the sound of Jackson crunching in the snow, of Ava's breath.

Actually, there was kind of a lot of snow. Ava looked down at her decidedly not-weather-proofed boots.

"Jackson?"

He had already gotten off of the snowmobile and was strapping the packages he'd brought with him to his back.

"Jackson, I don't know if these boots—"

He didn't answer except to lift her from the back of the snowmobile. He slung her around until he caught her legs and she was cradled in his arms.

Ava bit her lip. She loved being tossed around. "That's ok, too."

She thought she saw him smile in the dark, and then he carried her, not as far as it looked, just down a curved path and into a clearing that ended in what looked like a cliff. There was yellow light coming from below the edge of the cliff, lighting the smooth, flat rocks that emerged from under the snow near its edge.

"It's gorgeous," she said.

"You ain't seen nothing yet."

He carried her over to the smooth rocks on the very edge of the cliff and set her down.

"Stay there," he said. Then he started rummaging about in his pack, leaving Ava to look around, rooted to the spot.

She could see trees to either side, some quite close, and one with branches that hung over the edge of the cliff. Which, there was a cliff, and something below was lit...

The quarry pond. They must be above the quarry pond. It would be beautiful right now to look over the edge, but Jackson had told her to stay put. She would. She looked more immediately around her, and saw that the rocks were bare because someone had removed the snow and then placed several propane-powered outdoor heating lamps in what looked like a very strategic semi-circle. She was actually getting overheated in her parka.

"Take off the coat," Jackson said behind her. She

turned to find him messing about with some sort of complicated rope rig and froze, transfixed by what that implied.

"I said: take off the coat, Ava."

Her eyes still locked on those ropes, she complied. She wasn't even cold, surrounded by the heat lamps, but she shivered anyway.

"Put out your hands," he said, and walked towards her. He was lit very softly from below, from the light of the lanterns surrounding the quarry pond at the bottom of the cliff. It made him seem even more imposing. Ava extended both hands for him, wrists together. Somehow, she knew what he wanted.

He tied her wrists together with a length of rope, using some fancy knot Ava had never seen before. Her sweater dress provided some cushioning so the ropes didn't cut into her skin, but she wasn't getting free without help.

He led her by the length of rope closer to the edge of the cliff — very close, in fact. She could look down into the quarry if she bent over; on her tip toes, she could see the uneven snow cover on the blue ice, all of it surrounded by the glow of lanterns hanging from studs in the sheer rock walls.

"Stay where you are," he said again. He walked a few feet away and flung some sort of pulley-looking thing over the tree branch that extended out over the edge of the yawning quarry. Ava looked down and realized the line over the branch was the same one that bound her wrists.

She swallowed.

Jackson wasn't done. There was another contraption rigged to the first. He was busy for what seemed like a long time setting everything up—he even climbed the tree and did some sort of complicated looking things up there. Ava actually preferred not to pay attention. She guessed that if she tried to figure out what would happen and how, she'd be distracted when it actually came to pass.

Apparently it would involve rope.

She took a deep breath.

"Come here," he said, motioning her a step closer to the edge. She was just close enough to see down into the quarry, but not quite close enough to be afraid. He pulled on the line, and slowly the rope that bound her wrists began to grow taut, pulling her arms up and out, towards the edge of the cliff. Ava watched him nervously. He stopped with her arms raised just above her shoulders, pulled forward slightly at the waist. She wouldn't be able to walk in any direction but forward, and that was not an option for obvious, cliff-related reasons. She could see him grinning.

Ava began to breathe a little faster.

"Stay," he said, this time lightly. She cocked her head and made a face, an instinctual, sarcastic gesture that she instantly regretted.

Sort of.

He only slapped her ass once, but it sent thrilling vibrations through her whole body. "I'm not falling for your tricks, Ava," he said in her ear. "Next time, it really will be a punishment. Like not being allowed to come."

"I'm sorry," she said quickly.

He moved his hands down the sides of her legs and took hold of one ankle, moving it farther out to the side. Then he did the same to the other, spreading her legs a few feet apart. Even though she was fully clothed, it felt...vulnerable, with her body slightly bent at the waist. She had to arch her lower back slightly to keep her balance, pushing her ass up and out, like an invitation.

She clenched at the thought and looked down. He'd fastened ropes securely around the ankles of her laced boots. She followed the lines of rope; each went towards the trees, into the dark.

She was tied between two trees.

Ava closed her eyes and savored the feeling. Even fully clothed...

But Jackson was making some sort of noise behind her, going through that pack. She heard him crunch in the snow, heard a different sound when he reached the dry, flat area of rock. He was right behind her now. She could hear him breathing.

Why isn't he touching me? What is he –

First, she just felt the sweater dress pull against her neck at the collar line as he pulled it back, getting some slack away from her skin. Then it began to fall away from her body. There was a rough, grating sound of cloth separating, of wool, of her sweater dress...

Being cut off of her body.

Oh my God.

The sweater dress hung uselessly around her arms now, her back nearly naked to the night air and the heat of the lamps. There was a snapping sound, and her bra strap fell forward. She was bare. She heard a cutting sound to her left: he was slowly cutting down the length of the sleeve with a large knife, taking care to pull the fabric far away from her skin. She felt his breath on her bare skin, felt the warmth of the lamps and the chill of the winter air; she closed her eyes, and the dress was gone. She was naked from the waist up, her breasts already reacting, her nipples already pert.

When she opened her eyes, she didn't see him. For a wild moment, there was panic, and then there was a hand on her back, a large, calm hand, rubbing her up and down. She sighed, and he moved his hands around to her front, fondling each breast lovingly. He pinched both nipples at once, and laughed when she gasped.

Then she felt a pull on the waistband of her leggings. She held her breath while he cut them away from her body, first down one leg, then the other. With the same deliberate care, he cut the thin waistband of her panties, first one side, then the other, and she was naked. With a great sigh, she gasped for air, her whole body breathing in the cold night, the simultaneous chill of the winter air on her nakedness and the warmth from the lamps and just the very nearness of *him*…

She felt drunk. She wasn't drunk. She'd had only one glass of wine. What was this?

Where was Jackson?

She didn't know how long she stood there, naked and exposed and bound, before she became certain he was no longer near her. She was already feeling somehow outside of herself, feeling that time was distorted and sensation heightened. She couldn't be certain; she couldn't look behind her. It was just a feeling.

"Jackson?"

There was no answer.

Ava now felt the cold wind on her bare cunt, on the wetness there. The sharp sensation focused her entire awareness there for one second, and then it abated and her conscious mind regained some semblance of its normal faculties.

"Jackson?"

He wouldn't leave her out there, not tied and bare and vulnerable to anyone who came by. To any of the other guests. Any of the employees. Her entire abdomen tightened at the thought, and the heavy pulse between her legs told her she was swollen and ready. Why did that thought excite her so much? She knew she should be scared, but in the same way she knew random facts about the world, not as something real and immediate and *felt*...

She heard voices.

The awareness of other human beings nearby shot through her body like an electrical current. Exactly like a current. Once, on her best friend's grandparents' farm when she was a kid, she'd touched the mildly electrified fence that surrounded the horse paddock on a dare. Her whole body had become a kind of rigid, static fire, and her mind had gone blank. This was exactly like that.

She couldn't have moved, anyway. She was tied.

The wind rushed over her again, its cool caresses raising her nipples into hard, fine points, like the whole world was participating in this. Slowly, Ava's mind became aware of more salient facts: the voices, more than one, male and female, coming from below. They seemed loud because they were echoing off the high stone walls of the quarry.

The other guests had all been carrying ice skates…

She saw them begin to arrive, clambering down the rough stone steps that had been cut into the earth, gathering together on the wide stone platform that reached out into the frozen pond. If they looked up, they would see her. She would be well lit by the lanterns, the angle of the cliff as it sloped down into the pond providing them a full view of her naked body, bent over and bound. She would be completely exposed, even to the people she'd been hiding from earlier.

Ava began to shake. First her legs, then her arms, and finally, her core—all of it trembled. She didn't dare call out, didn't want to attract attention to herself, didn't want to be seen. Didn't want to be *known*. Oh God, more than anything else, she didn't want to be seen for what she was, with no way of controlling it, no way of presenting herself as she wanted to be seen. Where was Jackson? Why was this happening? Where…

This time, she heard the crunch of boots in the snow behind her. The furious trembling ceased, replaced only by the rapid sound of her breathing and the shouting laughter of the skaters below.

"Jackson?" she whispered, so softly she couldn't be sure that anyone but her could have heard. She was still so afraid of catching the attention of the skaters below, of being seen.

The crunch of boots grew closer, then stopped. Whoever it was must have been right behind her. *It must be Jackson…right? What if…*

Oh God, what if it isn't him?

The delighted shriek of a female skater from below stretched her mind as tight as the ropes that bound her: which thing did she fear more? Being seen, or the unknown man behind her? One of the men in her line of sight threw back his head in laughter, and Ava flinched. He could have seen her, and if one of them did, then they all—

A large, rough hand pressed into the small of her back, and her awareness of the world around her contracted into the small area of contact where the unknown man's skin touched hers. He rubbed the hand up her spine and down again, setting her whole body to trembling again.

He did not speak.

She was afraid to ask.

Her body reared with desire, her lower back straining to present herself to whomever was behind her. Her animal brain was taking over completely. Jackson had done exactly what he knew would drive her insane: left her bound, vulnerable, under someone else's control, and he'd done it in a place where she could be *seen*.

Oh God, she needed to get fucked. She needed Jackson.

Please, Jackson…

He wouldn't let her be left for anyone else; he wouldn't want her with anyone else—he'd *said* that, hadn't he?

"Jackson? *Oh God.*"

The man behind her thrust his hand between her spread legs, palming her ass with a large hand while his fingers stroked at her wet folds. Her leg began to shake again, an involuntary response, and her body strained against the rope that held her arms aloft as she tried to reach back to him. It was mindless. Before she knew it, she'd groaned aloud, and this brought her back slightly, reminded her there was some reason she hadn't called out, hadn't demanded, out loud, to know who was behind her, even though she was sure it had to be him, this had to be part of his plan, and then she looked down.

Part of his plan…

Nobody had heard her—yet. The skaters still chased each other around the pond. But if this continued, she wouldn't be able to hold it in. She would scream out into the night.

The man behind her seemed to read her thoughts. He pushed two fingers deep inside her, and she let out a surprised cry as her hips pushed into his hand and her arms pulled against the rope, her eyes flying wide open.

"Oh God…please…"

The man didn't answer except to reach around and rub one nipple, then the other, spreading a slick, smooth oil on her skin. As he reached down to her clit, a prickly warmth began to rise up on the surface of her skin where he'd spread the oil. She had just a moment to wonder what was in the oil before he thrust a third finger inside her and began to rub the remaining oil on her clit.

This time, she cried out.

She couldn't bear to look down, couldn't do much of anything besides fight off the pressure that was building inside her. She wasn't ready—she wasn't near ready to have a screaming orgasm in front of all of these people.

The man still held her, one hand in the front, the other in the back, his fingers working inside her.

She felt him lean close into her back, felt the itchy material of his sweater.

Jackson...

"Don't you fight me, Ava."

It was Jackson's voice, Jackson's low, dominant growl. She opened her eyes and looked up to the moon. His fingers swirled around her clit in a slow, steady, maddening rhythm. Soon she would be helpless to keep from coming. Her entire low body was contracting in anticipation, her insides coiled tight around the pressure.

"Think about what you learned so far. Don't fight that. You need to relax into me, just let it go. Go into that space. Do it now."

How did he know about that? About what it had felt like, tied down in his apartment, her legs spread? Like she'd shed all earthly concerns, existed only on a current of sensation and love and...

"This is what you're going to do, Ava: you're going to face your fear of being seen for what you are, and you're going to use it. You're going to take that feeling of being ashamed and afraid and turn it into something worthwhile while I fuck you. You will come hard, screaming loud enough for everyone to hear you and look up and see you getting fucked, and you're going to like it."

Ava closed her eyes again and felt herself slide into that place. It felt slow, but must have only been a few moments. His fingers were pushing and rubbing, each movement a burst of sensation, like a steady beacon guiding her toward a space where everything but the present fell away. She opened her eyes, looked down at the skaters below, and sighed.

Could she do it? She knew, suddenly, that she could. Somehow there was freedom in obedience. She could do this for him.

He pulled away from her, and the shock of it brought back the reality of being bound, of being tied between trees, of the rustling sounds of his clothing, of a zipper being undone, of the alternate extremes of cold air and warmth from the lamps. It was like her mind became unmoored, battered about with the sudden intrusion of the rest of the world, and there was a moment of sheer panic at the suddenness of it, at being off-balance —

He plunged into her with his cock, driving in deep, so deep and so quickly that she felt herself pushed forward against the ropes around her ankles, forcing her down against the ropes that held her wrists. She screamed, loudly, her eyes wide open.

The skaters all looked around. One looked up. Then they all looked up.

He grabbed her by the hips, massive fingers gripping her hip bones, thumbs digging into the tops of her buttocks, and pulled her back as he pushed forward, going deeper and deeper with every stroke. Everything disappeared except for the feeling of *him*, pounding into her, the oils *he* had rubbed on her, the sounds of *his* skin against hers.

"Keep your eyes open, Ava," he growled, and slowed his stroke, pulling out until she could only feel him at the very edge, until she missed being full of him, until she was desperate for it. How did he know?

She opened her eyes to see the skaters all

watching, all entertained, smiling broadly. One clapped, and gave her the thumbs-up sign. Days ago, she might have been destroyed by that; now she let it add a little spark to the sensations she already felt, let it add to the simple, animalistic joy she felt at being fucked by Jackson Reed. He made it into something else, made it safe for her to be bare. Nothing could hurt her; her vulnerability was now a boast, not a wound.

Like he knew, he bucked to her again, and this time, there was no stopping it. She started a slow, continuous cry as he plowed into her, her body refusing to be held at bay any longer. The pressure that had built up—so much pressure, as though it had been collecting for years—began to unfurl, slowly at first, then gathering steam. It was unlike any other orgasm she'd ever had, lashing at her, working its way up her body to a slow, steady beat until it reached her mind, and the echoes reverberated back down her spine, all the way to her core, and the resonance blew her apart.

She had no memory of what happened next.

She supposed she screamed.

She supposed he came inside her. She supposed he cut her down, carefully, wrapped her in the parka, and carried her back from the edge.

When she came to, fully, her brain still kind of foggy, her mouth still not working properly, he was holding her in his lap while he leaned back against a tree. He'd brought a heat lamp and cleared the snow, and there was both water and wine and a little picnic basket nearby. The rocky place where she'd been bound and fucked was not fifteen feet away.

Jackson was brushing her hair, caressing her face, her neck with his large, gentle fingers. She turned toward his hand on her cheek and instinctively kissed it. He tilted her face up to his, which was dark and unknowable with the moon behind his head.

"Hey," he said, his voice catching. "I'm so proud of you."

She didn't know what she had expected to hear, but it wasn't that. She pulled at his sweater, and he bent down to kiss her. It felt...perfect.

Jackson took care of her for a long time, feeding her a little food, making her drink water. And when he decided she was ready to move, he helped her get into some comfy sweats he'd brought, wrapped her back in that warm parka, and carried her back to the sled. He even carried her back inside, all the way to their room, and put her to bed. But not once did she feel weak, or incapable. Instead, the whole time she felt mighty and strong, and she even, for a brief moment, allowed herself to feel loved.

But it would last less than a day.

chapter 13

Jackson woke up slowly. He didn't move for a long time. Ava was sleeping peacefully, curled up against his chest, and he didn't want that to change. Besides, he needed some time to take it all in in the light of day. That had been the most intense scene he'd ever done.

He'd never been so hopped up before a scene, either. It wasn't like him. Just wasn't. And it wasn't that he'd doubted the outcome, or his judgment, or Ava. It just...*mattered* more. More than anything he wanted to give her release from the pressure that she felt from whatever it was that she was so afraid of. Even if he didn't feel he owed her everything, which he absolutely knew he did, he would still want to help ease that burden. It hurt him to watch her carry it. And maybe if he could help her to overcome it, in steps, eventually she would tell him about it.

He tried not to think about the fact that,

technically, he only had a week.

And it did trouble him that she was even more guarded now than she had been then. Though he supposed that shouldn't be such a great shock. Ten years was a long time, with plenty of opportunities to get hurt all over again. He had no idea where he'd be if it hadn't been for what Ava had given him.

With a cute little sigh, Ava half woke up, grabbed one of his hands, rolled over with her bare ass against his already-hard cock, and hugged his arm to her chest, right up against her breasts.

If Jackson were any other kind of man, he might have suffered in silence. But he wasn't. He was who he was, and Ava was his sub, and they had an arrangement.

Those breasts were his to play with if he felt like it, and he felt like it.

"Hey," Ava said, sleep still thick on her tongue.

"You knew what you were doing," he said into her hair, and tweaked a nipple.

That woke her up. She wiggled her bottom and made a satisfied little noise when she discovered how hard he was. He rolled her breasts lazily in his hand, not in a hurry to rush. She pressed her ass into him a little harder, and he chuckled.

"Nuh uh," he said.

She half turned, and he could see her frown in the way her brow furrowed.

"Relax," he said. "I just decided that you should beg first."

She tried to turn over, he was sure to swat at him, but he caught her wrists and moved them up above her head. He knew she liked that. In a just a moment, he shifted his weight and brought his other arm around and under her neck and transferred her wrists from one hand to the other. That left him free to play with his right hand while she was pinned on her side. The first thing he did was get another handful of her luscious breasts.

Her breathing quickened, and he could feel her getting wet already. They were so perfectly matched. Right now, he couldn't think of anything hotter than Ava, held under him, wanting him, and he would've given good odds that she would say the same.

"What do you say?" he said.

"Mmm, I don't know." She was trying to sound nonchalant. She hadn't succeeded. He felt her chest rising rapidly under his hand, knew she was getting hot.

He moved his hand down and pulled away the sheet, uncovering her naked body. Then he slapped the side of her ass, hard. She giggled, and buried her face in the pillow. She was breathing even harder now.

God*damn* she was beautiful. He wished she wouldn't hide her face.

"What do you say?" he asked again, and then gave her another good slap.

He heard her smile in her tone. "What was the question again?"

"Oh, that's it," he said, and rolled her over on her stomach to spank her properly. She stretched out her whole body under him, squirming in anticipation, and as she turned her face to the side, he saw a big, dumb grin on her face.

Well, then.

He sat up, still pinning her wrists down tight, threw one leg over her, and spanked her from right to left, left to right, then back again. She let out something between a giggle, a squeal, and a moan every time he struck her. He could listen to that all day.

"Now what do you say?" he said, slipping his hand between her tight thighs and lifting off of her so she had room to spread.

She let out a long, slow sigh, pushed her ass up off the bed like a gift, and said, "Please."

He could have fucked her like that, driving her face into that pillow until she couldn't hardly stand it, covering them both with sweat and giving her a good start to the day.

"Turn over," he said.

She looked over her shoulder, confused.

"Turn over," he said, this time softly. He helped her roll back over, lifted one leg and got around it so he lay between her legs. She looked up at him, her eyes wide and a bit concerned, like she thought she'd done something wrong.

"I just want to see you," he said, and brushed her long hair out of her face. "That's all."

As soon as he said it, he felt the risk. Felt like he'd just let fly something fragile, felt like there was a great distance between him and the ground, and no guarantee that she'd catch the line. But it was true. He didn't want to pretend it wasn't. He had to *see* her while he was inside her, and know she knew he could see her, and he wanted her to know how much it meant to him. Just this once, just right now. He wouldn't make her talk about it, not yet.

"That's an order," he said softly.

She pressed her lips together, her eyes big and blue and surprised, though Ava almost never let herself look surprised, as though surprise was a sign of weakness. He knew she wouldn't speak, but after a moment, she nodded. He leaned down and kissed her on the forehead, then the tip of her nose, then her lips. By the time he had moved to her throat, she was smiling again, and her body writhed underneath him. Her breasts rose to meet his mouth, and she wrapped one leg around his waist, trying to pull him into her.

That was enough for him.

He rose, positioned himself with the head of his aching cock right at the entrance to her vagina, and planted his two arms on either side of her. Her blue eyes got big again, but she didn't shy away. She met his eyes. And he slowly, slowly, slowly pushed into her.

Inch by incredible, soft, warm, wet inch, he watched her face. He got to watch every sensation play across her features, got to watch as the pleasure built and her defenses faded away, got to see that, at her very core, underneath it all, as she was about to come while blinking back tears, Ava Barnett did love him.

Even if she didn't know it yet, even if she wouldn't say it yet. She loved him.

He rocked her to another orgasm, and then let himself loose inside her.

~ ~ ~

After they'd made love in the bright morning light, Jackson had sensed that he needed to give her some space. Granted, it had taken him a minute. He'd been completely spent, not just physically, but emotionally. He'd thought the scene above the pond was intense, but Christ, Ava brought intense to a new level just by being Ava.

He'd come to his senses still lying on top of her, sweaty and exhausted, and with the unmistakable impression that she was also coming to, and might need to do it without two hundred pounds of former football player on top of her.

He'd kissed her, and then he'd kissed her again, and then he'd done it again, until he was sure she knew how much he meant it. Then he'd gotten up for a shower with his fingers crossed that she wouldn't put too much distance between them when he got back.

If only.

Jackson came back into the bedroom to find Ava sitting up on the side of the bed, the sheet wrapped around her, cell phone pinned to her ear. When she saw him come in, she turned away, her voice lowered.

"What do you mean, you don't want me to be blindsided?" Ava tried to whisper and yell into her phone at once. It didn't quite work. "Spit it out, Ellie!"

Jackson's mind churned. Ellie was her sister, her kid sister. The one she was always crazy protective over. Ellie had been in high school during Ava's senior year at college. Six years apart. Maybe seven? At the time, it had seemed like a big gap. It must have seemed even bigger when they were kids. Jackson had always had the distinct sense that Ava had been protecting Ellie since the day Ellie was born, but he'd never quite worked out from what or how. Well, from their mother — that much was obvious. Their father was dead. But what specific kind of harm Ava was afraid their mother might inflict upon Ellie was a mystery.

"Say that again," Ava said into the phone, her voice flat. She didn't bother to try to hide her voice this time.

Jackson toweled off his hair quickly and wiped his body down. No point in letting her know he was listening, paying attention, studying. Give her some semblance of privacy. It wasn't like she couldn't have gone to another room if she'd really wanted that privacy, anyhow. He grinned. Ava was the queen of self-sabotage. It would be just like her to sabotage her own efforts at holding a man she cared about at arm's length.

This is not the time to laugh, Reed.

He set about dressing quickly, figuring he'd heard all he needed to hear. She'd tell him the rest if she felt like it. He didn't have to wait long. He heard her say goodbye, and then turned to find her just sitting, motionless, on the bed they'd just shared.

It nearly broke his heart.

He regretted putting clothes on now. He felt like skin to skin would be best, given the circumstances. He climbed across the bed, pulling his shirt over his head as he did so, and wordlessly pulled her into his arms from behind. He didn't say anything. Just buried his face in her neck and held her.

After a moment, he realized she was trying not to cry. She'd be mortified if he noticed. He tried to give her cover.

"So who was that?" He said it as coolly as he could.

"Ellie."

"How's she doing?"

He pretended he didn't feel her shoulders shudder, and just held her tighter.

"You should see that shower, by the way," he said. "Even better than mine. In fact, I might have to get in there with you."

He nuzzled her neck and she laughed a little, which was an improvement, except that right at the end, a sob tried to get out. She nearly choked herself with the effort of holding it back. His heart broke a little more. He didn't know why she felt she couldn't cry in front of him when they always seemed to get each other in every other situation, but maybe now was not the time to argue that particular point.

"How 'bout those Jets, huh?" he said.

Now she laughed. They'd gone to a Jets game together in college. Ironically, it had been a sobering experience.

"Ava—" he started, but she was quick on the draw and didn't let him finish.

"It's nothing," she said, and wiped her eyes with her head turned away, as though he didn't know that meant she'd been crying. "My mother is getting married."

It wasn't until she'd said that that Jackson realized he'd had a number of scenarios in mind. Death in the family, disease, unwanted pregnancy, God forbid some kind of assault. But he hadn't, for the life of him, expected to hear that a wedding was the problem.

Jackson turned her around, saw the confused expression she had going on, equal parts panic and grief and a whole lot of bewildered anger on top, and thought: *Does she even know why she's crying?* The woman who famously saw through other people, right to their core, couldn't see her own self? It was almost funny, in an incredibly unfunny way.

"Ava," he said.

"I don't want to talk about it." He handed her a tissue, and she snatched it out of his hand.

"No shit," he said, feeling hurt. "You never do."

It was like he'd slapped her. She looked at him, stunned.

You're pushing her too far, Reed. Not the right time. Even so, Jackson felt his own frustration start to crest inside him, and, fuck it, they had been so *close*. He just wanted to stop managing everything, for once, just say what was on his mind.

"Why?" he said. "Why the hell is your mother getting married a freaking tragedy?"

Oh, fuck. He hadn't meant to belittle her feelings, just show that he didn't understand. And probably being pissed that she hadn't immediately told him everything wasn't a great idea, either. He wanted to keep talking to try to fix it, but nothing he actually wanted to say was helpful. Instead, the controlled Dom part of him heard what he said next with disgust.

"Ava, just fucking *tell* me. Haven't I shown you it's better to be open and honest about stuff?"

She blinked at him, then carefully got up from the bed and started opening drawers.

Fuck.

"You've shown me a lot of kinky sex after a decade of nothing. The sex has been fantastic, by the way," she added, almost as an afterthought. *Ouch.* "But it was just sex. It doesn't change anything about the last ten years, and it doesn't change anything about the life I had before I ever knew you."

He shot up from the bed and grabbed hold of her arm, spinning her around. It was suddenly very clear that neither of them was wearing many clothes. "Please look at me," he said.

He was profoundly conscious of her nakedness, of the heat that was always there between them, like a natural force that pulled them together. They stared at each other, fuming, for what seemed like a long time.

"That's not true," he finally said. "It's more than that, I know you felt it. What we have can change…things."

She smiled, her cheeks dry and her eyes cold.

"Really?" she said. "You chat much about your family today?"

He had no response. That didn't stop Ava from pressing forward.

"And if I did tell you all about it, Jackson, if I told you the most private things, what would you do? Do you think you would hold me, and I'd cry, and then it would all work out? *Somehow*?"

Jackson hadn't ever seen her angry, really, not like this. He hadn't realized…

"Or," she said, her voice dropping to bitterness, "would you just look at me with that stupid, horrified, open-mouthed look, and let me know exactly what you thought of me? Like last time?"

There it was. He didn't know what to say. Maybe that's why he hadn't said anything, why he hadn't started out with an apology and an explanation: there was none, not without talking about things that maybe *he* didn't love talking about. Of course he didn't want to tell her about his family; he wanted her to like him.

He felt sadness fall around him like a dull rain. "I wanted to show you that you could trust me," he said, sitting back on the bed, his big, useless hands held open in his lap.

"It's not your fault, Jackson," she said, and she started to get dressed. "Though you're being a total ass right now. I get that stuff can work out, that it's possible, or whatever. I've just never seen it happen, and I don't feel like there's a whole lot of reason… I just don't like those odds, considering the payoff."

He winced. She was almost done getting dressed now. It felt like the final seconds ticking down on the game clock.

"You're wrong, Ava."

Ava turned and put on the final bits of her armor in full view of him. She was calm, perfectly calm, about a hundred times more calm than he felt.

"This is not something with a wrong or right answer," she said gently. "It's a choice."

"It's the wrong choice."

"But it's mine."

He rose, suddenly furious. It was still *wrong*, so obviously, clearly wrong, a goddamn *child* could see that. She was fucking up her life—what should have been *their* life—for no good reason. The familiar anger crept up on him, that anger he hadn't felt in years, anger at good people making bad decisions that hurt them, and him as a bonus. He felt it radiate out from his chest to his arms, his legs...

Jackson suddenly saw her, again, standing in front of him. For the first time, she looked a little afraid.

He opened and closed his fists.

"Of course it's your choice, Ava," he said. "But you're still wrong. About the payoff. You are dead wrong about that."

"I'm leaving, Jackson." He hated how she said it tentatively. Like she was worried about how he would react.

"I know. Am I going to see you again?"

She actually looked at him with pity. "I don't know."

chapter 14

It took Ava over half an hour to get herself into the restaurant. She'd been trudging through the snow the whole time. She had taken a cab in that kind of weather, like a normal person, and had gotten out at 6th Avenue, perfectly willing to walk the half-block to the shitty chain Chinese restaurant in the middle of Midtown. But as she'd gotten closer, looking up occasionally from the slippery, slush-covered sidewalk, a feeling of foreboding had gathered around her, increasing in density until she just couldn't bear it any longer.

When she'd actually gotten to the restaurant, she'd just kept walking.

Now it had been at least thirty minutes , she was late, and she was frozen to the bone after walking the same four blocks, over and over again, circling around the place like a drain.

Christmas dinner with her mother. Jesus fucking Christ.

Probably not the ideal day to take the Lord's name in vain. But it wasn't the first time that day, and it probably wouldn't be the last.

Really, what was there to look forward to? She'd seen this exact scenario play out a hundred times before — her mother and the boyfriend *du jour* — and it never went well. A comedy, this was not. She wondered how many drinks her mom had put away already. Would she still be sweet-drunk when Ava finally worked up the courage to walk in there? Or would she already have slid all the way into mean-drunk?

The woman was getting *married*. Ava shook her head.

In the end, the only thing that impelled her into the restaurant was the thought of Ellie alone with their mother. That had always been something that could reliably send Ava's adrenaline into overdrive. She mentally kicked herself, wishing she'd had the brains to deal with her mom days ago and had just told Ellie to stay home. If she hadn't been distracted by Jackson, she would have.

No. Do NOT think about Jackson Reed.

Too late. Lump in her throat.

It turned out she'd rather face her mother than think about Jackson, which was quite an accomplishment for the guy. Ava pushed open the huge wooden doors.

The world seemed to fall away a little bit as she went through the motions. Ava knew she spoke to the coat check girl, but she couldn't have remembered what was said. She couldn't have told anyone what music was playing. She was falling into that familiar, protective place she reserved for time spent around her mother, where everything was just a dull echo of its normal self.

She saw Ellie first, seated in a red leather booth facing the door. That snapped Ava right back to reality. She couldn't afford to slip into the protective cocoon if it meant leaving Ellie by herself.

Ellie waved. Her sister looked…strangely optimistic? A little nervous, maybe, but not desperate, not hurt.

Ava didn't wait to catch her mother's eye. She started threading her way through the sea of tables as soon as she saw that blonde, coiffed head begin to turn her in her direction.

"Hey you," Ellie said, smiling up at her. Ava already felt terrifically guilty, as she should. She'd been walking in circles in the snow while her kid sister had, as always, been on time. Ava smiled weakly back, trying to apologize with her eyes, and steeled herself for what came next.

"Merry Christmas, Ava." Her mother, Patricia, had half-risen from her seat, as though unsure if she should hug her daughter. It caught Ava off-guard, and they met in a sort of scrunched half back pat. Ava hurried over to the other side of the booth and scooted in next to her sister.

Something was different. Something was off. Her mother's hesitant, almost apologetic smile was unlike anything Ava had ever seen before. For one, she was completely sober. That was ice water in front of Patricia. And two, she seemed…self-aware.

Ava was on high alert.

"Hi, Mom."

Her mother let out a nervous laugh, like she'd

been holding her breath until Ava spoke. She covered her mouth with one hand and reached for her water glass with the other.

The one with the big, fat stinking engagement ring on it.

"So I hear you're getting married," Ava said.

"Ava," Ellie said softly.

"Yes," Patricia said. She looked at Ava, but Ava just couldn't meet her eyes.

She just couldn't stop staring at that ring.

Ava didn't know how to explain how she was feeling, not even to herself. She knew that not even Ellie, who'd been there for the worst of it, could possibly know what she was feeling. Looking at that ring, knowing what it represented, it was impossible not to think about all the other times Patricia had told her eldest daughter that she'd met a man, that this one was The One. That usually meant that Patricia would become nice, and funny, and interested, and loving, and basically the best mom on the planet, because she was happy. That was when she was Ava's best friend. That was when they'd spend happy afternoons together, making up stories, painting, putting on musicals to entertain Ellie. At night, Patricia would go out with her boyfriend, but it was with the promise of even more happiness later.

And then, of course, there was what happened next. What always, always happened next.

Patricia looked from one daughter to the other, her eyes darting between them like a frightened bird.

"I think I should give you two a moment," Patricia said quietly. "I'll just go to the ladies' room."

Ava exhaled, felt herself deflate as she watched her mother walk away from the table. She already felt tired.

Ellie said dryly, "You don't seem entirely happy for Mom."

"You don't remember when it was really bad, El. What she was like."

"Oh, I dunno," Ellie said, reaching for her own water. "I probably remember more than you'd think. I remember the yelling."

Ava made a face. "The yelling."

"I remember once—or, I don't know if it was just once—but she tore up these pictures that we'd made. They were really nice—that's what I remember—and she tore them up."

"It was more than once."

Ellie smiled. "Well, if she found a good move, she wasn't going to let it go to waste."

"God forbid."

"And I remember her saying no one would ever love us…"

"…the way she did."

"She hit you sometimes."

There was a pause. Generally, by mutual agreement, the Barnett sisters didn't talk about this part of their childhood. But this seemed like a special occasion.

Ellie downed her glass. "She did *not* handle break ups well."

Ava laughed. She kept laughing for no real reason—it wasn't funny, not really—right up until their mother returned to the table, nervous as ever. Ava couldn't remember her mother ever being nervous before. She had always been a charming flirt who could make anyone feel like the center of the universe. This woman in front of her was like some sort of pod person. She wanted to shake her mom, tell her to stop the act, to be real. The whole thing made her so damn anxious, and now she didn't even have time to ask Ellie what she knew about this supposed marriage.

"Those bathrooms are fabulous," Patricia said.

Ava had nothing for that. Ellie smiled at their mother encouragingly.

"Ok, I can't take this," Ava suddenly said, sitting up straight. "What the hell is this about getting married?"

"He's actually a nice guy, Ava," Ellie said.

Ava looked at her, betrayed. "You've *met* him?"

"I met Dave in AA," Patricia said quietly. She smiled hesitantly at her eldest again. Ava hadn't even known her mother had quit drinking, let alone gone to AA. "He's been sober twenty-five years. He'd be here, but he's volunteering for the Samaritans tonight. They get really busy this time of year."

And, for the first time, Patricia Barnett let a hint of pride into her voice.

The conversation, such as it was, smoothed out after that. Patricia seemed to find her footing, Ellie was sweet, good-natured, witty Ellie, and Ava was at least on autopilot enough that she didn't just sit there like a dumb lump.

She felt like a dumb lump.

All of the different parts of her brain appeared to be working separately, and none of them were talking to each other. Whichever part was in charge of getting her to respond to small talk seemed to be operating just fine, but behind the scenes? Rationally, Ava knew she should be happy for her mother. To finally find health and happiness after all those years—years that had been hard on all of them—was obviously a great, great thing.

The thing was, nowhere inside her could Ava find even a little bit of happiness. All she found was anger. It didn't take Freud to figure out that Ava's issues with vulnerability and her inability to trust the world to not suck might have something to do with her mom being a crazy bitch for most of her life, and now that same mom got to have her own happily ever after while Ava herself was so hobbled by those issues that she fucked up every small shot she ever had at a real relationship.

How was that fair?

Ava wasn't stupid or crazy; she knew life was better with love in it. But it didn't seem like something she could count on. And now her mother, of all people, had found it, and Ava was doomed to a life spent alone, pushing people away.

People like Jackson.

Oh God. Jackson.

Even as Ava tried to ride out the silent storm that raged within her, all that anger and sadness and whatever the hell else was going on in there, the only person she wanted to be around was Jackson freaking Reed. He would get it. She could make jokes between tears if she wanted, and he would get it, and he wouldn't...

He would *get* it.

And she'd just said a bunch of horrible things to him and left him, because he'd tried to be there for her, even if he'd been a jerk about it.

"I think I'm going to throw up," Ava announced.

Her mother and sister were even more surprised when Ava didn't run for the bathroom, but for the door.

chapter 15

Jackson had been blessed with singularity of purpose from about five minutes after Ava had left the Volare estate until about five minutes after he'd found himself standing outside her dingy walk up apartment building in Alphabet City. He knew he *had* been blessed, because — very, very suddenly — it was gone.

Now he was just an idiot standing in the snow, wondering if he was a stalker.

He was frustrated by the uncertainty in all of this. It wasn't that he was unused to ambiguity. He dealt in algorithms and languages and art, where ambiguity was almost a feature of expression, not a bug. But he was a decisive kind of man, a man who knew who he was and what he wanted and what he believed to be within the bounds of acceptable behavior — or, at least, he had worked very hard to become such a man.

Anyway, none of that helped him figure out if

showing up on Ava's doorstep with some snow-covered flowers and an apology was sweet as all get out or creepy as hell. At least there was no doorman to give him dirty looks.

Yeah, *that* made him feel better. He didn't like the looks of this building, and Alphabet City, while just trendy enough to be a little bit expensive, still had an unacceptable number of stabbings, as far as he was concerned. It was not the kind of place where he wanted Ava to live.

Maybe don't lead with that possessive stuff, Reed. Apologies first.

Only Ava could make him feel stupid. Only Ava could make him feel dumb enough and angry enough that he pushed ahead and said and did things because he felt like it, even if his brain knew it was a terrible idea. It was the worst kind of boundary to cross, and the fact that he loved her didn't excuse it. Of course she'd run away when he'd pushed her; he was probably *frightening*. He'd seen it coming. And he hadn't been able to stop himself.

"Fuck!" he said out loud to no one in particular.

"Yup," said a homeless guy huddled in the shadows next to Ava's stoop, bundled up in the remains of several different coats and covered in a light dusting of snow. Jackson hadn't even noticed he was there. He felt like a total asshole.

"Is there a shelter you can go to, man? Something nearby? It's cold as shit out here tonight," Jackson said, stomping his feet to feel his cold toes.

The guy shook his head, snow falling on his shoulders. "Don't like those places. I got my heating grate. What're you doing out here?"

Jackson looked at the flowers, now frozen solid. "Trying not to fuck up," he said.

The man on the grate laughed. "Good luck."

Jackson was thinking about how he'd already had more luck than he deserved in his short lifetime, and how Ava was by far the biggest part of it, when his phone rang.

It was her.

"Where are you?" She sounded stressed.

"Out buying ice cream," he lied. "Are you ok? Where are you?"

"I'm at your apartment. I needed..." Her voice, tiny and fragile sounding, trailed off. "I need to see you. Ok? Right now. Please?"

"I'll be right there, Ava. Don't move. Don't...don't go anywhere."

There was a pause, and the crackle of the snow-addled reception rang loud in his ear as he ran out onto Avenue B, intending to jump in front of the first cab he saw.

"I won't," she said.

Two cabs vied for Jackson's fare. He dug out just enough money for the ride back to his apartment in the West Village out of his coat pockets, shed the coat, and threw it at the guy sitting on the grate. It was a tiny gesture, but it was all he could get away with right now.

"What're you doing man?" the guy said. "This is a nice coat."

"You wished me good luck," Jackson said, ducking into the cab. "I got some."

~ ~ ~

Clive, the doorman, tried to apologize for letting Ava up.

"I've seen her here before, Mr. Reed, and she looked up upset, and..." He spread his hands out, like it just couldn't be helped. "It just seemed like the right thing."

"Yeah, she has that effect on people," Jackson said. "Upset?"

"Crying."

Shit.

Which was why Jackson wasn't prepared to see Ava pacing across the living room when he came in, biting her fingernails, then heading right for him and knocking him dead with a smoldering kiss.

Hell, not just smoldering. Like she really *meant* it.

She finally slid off his chest, arms unwrapping, breathing returning to normal. Now he could see that she really had been crying. Ava Barnett was one of those fortunate women who somehow looked good even when crying. It made her look vulnerable—one of the only times she allowed that to happen.

"What happened?" he said. She didn't answer him, her eyes already focused on something far away. He wasn't going to lose her again, not already. He took her arm and spun her around. "Ava! What happened?"

She pressed her lips together in that way that meant there was something she was trying not to say, and shook her head a tiny bit. "Not yet," she said. She seemed sad about it.

"Then what?" He felt frustration start to rise in his throat, and to stave it off, he put his hand at the back of her neck, lifting her face to look at him. He needed to feel her skin or he was going to lose his mind. "Ava, what do you want?"

"The payoff," she said, barely audible. "You said the payoff of trusting someone…was worth it."

"It is."

"Please show me," she said.

She said it so simply, without any irony. She was begging. Jackson could see that she struggled in that way that was peculiar to Ava, struggling against herself and every instinct she had to run and hide. Her mind and her heart were never going to lead the way. Her mind was too quick, and her heart was too scarred. Her body needed to show her. She needed to be dominated.

He gripped her hair at the back of her head, getting her full attention. Then he very slowly felt his way down the entire front of her body until he pushed his hand between her legs and grabbed her there.

"You're mine, Ava," he said, and watched her begin to sink into him, watched her sink into submission with palpable relief. This was where she should be. This was right. He would show her. He knew just the thing, something he hadn't wanted to do with anybody else.

"Take off your clothes," he said.

chapter 16

Ava's hands shook as she fumbled with the buttons on her tailored oxford. She wasn't nervous, exactly—it was like that time she'd gone rock climbing and her leg had started pumping uncontrollably. They'd told her it was adrenaline.

Whatever it was, it made her too slow. Jackson reached up and pulled the shirt open, sending a button flying.

"Faster," he said.

She'd never seen him like this. It fit; it was what she needed. The intensity, the razor sharp focus. She felt like nothing else in the world mattered to him but her. Like he couldn't even see anything else. His grey eyes were on fire.

"*Faster,*" he growled, and her fingers began to fly. That voice was not something to be disobeyed. It triggered something in her, something from prehistory, something primal.

She tore off her remaining clothes and stood

naked, shuddering. He had this way of...*looking* at her.

"Ava, we're going to have to go a little further," he said. "You're not going to have the option of keeping anything from me. Don't try."

His words passed over her bare skin, bringing it to life. Yes. That...that was what she needed. She couldn't do it on her own. Running out into the snow, realizing that everyone else was somehow capable of this, of finding another human being and making a bond with them, of letting go and letting them in, everyone except her — Ava realized Jackson would have to *make* her do it.

He was her only shot.

And she was so grateful to see that he understood that.

"I'm going to do things to you that require you to trust me completely," he said, stepping so close that she felt covered by his body. "You're going to be scared, and I'm going to do it anyway, and then I'm going to fuck you."

Almost casually, he reached between her legs, his favorite place, and then pulled back on her hair so she had to look up into his face. "You are going to have to surrender, Ava. Give it up completely. You understand?"

"Yes," she said.

"Good," he said, slapping her bare ass. "But first, I have to get you warmed up."

He walked away from her, sucking on his finger where it had been between her legs, and reached for the phone to the front desk downstairs. She was bereft without him, already feeling herself more grounded, more connected to the world around her when some part of him was inside her. "What do I do?" she asked, lost.

He let her hang on his silence, his hand resting on the phone. Then he said, "You get yourself off for me while I make arrangements."

"While you're on the phone?"

He picked it up, pressing the button. "I'd say you have a minute or two."

Jackson didn't say what would happen if she refused. He didn't have to. Ava was already swimming in the peculiar kind of freedom that had one singular focus: where disappointing him in anything at all would be painful.

But she had never done this before. She'd never masturbated to orgasm in front of anyone else. She realized it sort of belatedly; wasn't she kind of old to have never done something like this? But then again, this would be one person, watching her at her most vulnerable.

Of course she'd never done it before. The thought of it in the abstract was horrifying. The thought of it while looking at Jackson, under his orders...

Tentatively, she lifted one leg and positioned her foot on the rung of one of his kitchen bar stools. Her leg shook slightly. If she was going to be bare, she should be *bare*.

Jackson locked eyes with her. "Don't look away," he said.

Slowly, delicately at first, she began to touch herself. Instinctively, she wanted to close her eyes, to lose herself in the feeling, but there was Jackson's command. His eyes never left hers.

"Clive?" he said into the phone. "Remember

that deal we talked about? Yeah, unfettered access. About an hour or so. And I'd need the security cameras turned off. See if you can, I'll hold."

She was already wet, so wet, and suddenly she remembered she had only a minute or two—that's what he'd said. She pressed down on her clit, biting her own lip to keep from moaning, and rubbed the wet hood against the bundle of nerves in tight little circles, faster and faster, staring at Jackson's fiery eyes until she realized she was almost begging him, she didn't know for what, but pleading with him. She blinked tears out of her eyes, the kinds of tears that came when you couldn't think words, and a small orgasm ricocheted through her body in short little spurts that pushed her back against the counter while his eyes bored into hers.

She felt the first layers of sweat on her brow. She'd given him a part of herself, and she still stood there, naked, in offering. His.

Very much his.

"Thank you," Jackson said, and replaced the receiver. Then, without taking his eyes off her, he crossed the kitchen and pulled her to him by her wrist. He let her feel the length of him against her for just a beat, and then he kissed her.

"Thank *you*," she said when he let her go. She found she was still breathing heavily. She looked down to find her flat stomach twitching, her whole body still primed.

"Ava," he said sharply, and she looked up. She'd broken eye contact. "You're not done. Go to the chest and bring me the blue vibe, the smaller red vibe, and the riding crop."

Ava did not hesitate, and that surprised her. Her

constantly churning, questioning mind was finally starting to slow down, to ease itself. To just let her be. This was what she'd begun to find so addictive about these scenes with Jackson, with this part of...whatever they were. These moments when he seized all control and she could let go.

She opened the chest and swallowed. The blue vibe was curved, textured, and *large*. The red one was smaller, and flared, and...could only be for one thing.

And, of course, the riding crop.

Her overactive mind attempted to revolt. She quelled it and delivered the vibrators to Jackson. He took them and eyed them appreciatively.

"We have some time before everything is ready," he said, almost to himself. "And goddamn, do you need to get fucked."

Every muscle in her body tightened. He noticed, and a satisfied smile flickered across his face.

"Bend over the counter."

Ava nodded and walked to the kitchen counter. It was a proper counter from the living room side, but it was at about waist height from the kitchen side, perfect for bending over. She didn't realize she was dragging out her steps, walking slowly to savor how odd she was beginning to feel, until she felt Jackson behind her. He leaned forward and placed the vibes on the counter. Then he put his hand around the back of her neck, his other on her hip, and forcefully bent her over the counter. Her cheek pressed into the cold slate, and the vibes came in and out of focus, the only other things she could see.

Where was the riding crop?

"Spread," he said.

She did. Her breasts hurt a little, pressed into the cold stone, and she was getting wetter every time she tried to move under his hold and found she couldn't.

Powerless.

He stepped back, but kept his hold on her neck, and placed his boot between her legs to keep them wide open. He slid an easy finger into her, and swirled it around, as though hollowing her out.

"Do you remember what I said about discipline, Ava?"

"Yes," she breathed. "No. I don't know."

"I said you would obey my orders, and accept my discipline. Did you do that?"

Ava's mind reeled, but it was, as always, difficult to think with his finger inside her. It was like there was only room for so much at once.

"Yes," she said.

She felt the bulk of his body move away, though he kept his heavy hand on her neck. She was about to ask what she'd done wrong when she felt the sharp sting of the riding crop on her bare buttock.

"No," he said.

The stiff leather of the crop began to trace the lines of her inner thighs.

"You disobeyed me, Ava. Don't lie." The sudden crack of the riding crop streaked across her thighs, her buttocks, even close to her exposed sex. She whimpered, but not because she hurt. She liked the hurt.

"Tell me how," he said. The leather tip of the crop probed her wet slit, and she moaned.

"I ran away," she said.

"You ran away from me," he said, close to her ear now, and she suddenly saw that the blue vibe was gone. "And you're mine."

He buried the vibrator in her as far as it would go. She let out a short, convulsive breath that turned into a groan, the shock and slight pain of being so suddenly full quickly overwhelmed by the pleasure of the same. He fucked her leisurely with the vibe in long, slow strokes until she was reaching out across the countertop for something to grab hold of. And then...

He stopped.

"Oh, no," she cried. She had been so close, a deep orgasm building on top of her first of the night, and now she was teetering, on the brink of falling back still tight and wound and hungry.

"You won't come again until I tell you to, Ava," he whispered in her ear. He jiggled the vibrator inside her just once, as if to tease her, and then pulled it out.

She moaned her frustration, slapped a palm on the countertop. She heard him laugh. Then she felt it: a cold, cool, lube-covered finger, gently circling her anus.

"Jackson—"

"Shh," he said, and his grip on her neck tightened.

Ava closed her eyes and tried to relax. This wasn't something she was used to. His finger felt good on the delicate skin, the nerves alive in a way that she hadn't expected. He pushed against her with more and more pressure until he finally forced his finger in. Her eyes shot open; it felt intrusive, invasive, wrong, but in all the right ways. He began to fuck her ass with his finger, curling it around and circling it to stretch her out.

He added more lube, and then another finger, and she moaned helplessly.

"Don't come, Ava," he warned.

She whimpered, and nodded as best she could with her cheek pressed into the counter. It was just becoming manageable when, all at once, he removed his fingers and replaced them with the tip of something much larger.

The red vibe.

It hadn't looked that big—it hadn't looked big at all—but now, pressed against her tight sphincter, it felt impossibly huge. She tried to shake her head, to lift it off the counter; it was just too big, there was no…

"Oh, God!"

She cried out as he pushed it past the tight ring of muscle. She felt a slight pop, and then it was in. It felt…she didn't have words. Every move rubbed it against some new bundle of nerves, some part of her body that had never known pleasure. It was a constant, invasive reminder of his dominance.

"Stay like that, Ava."

And then he was gone.

She saw him walk past her line of sight, past the counter. Heard him walk through the living room and into his bedroom. Heard him close the door. She was still bent flat over the counter, her bottom slightly tilted up, and now with a red vibe sticking out of her. She didn't dare move. After a while, she found she didn't even want to; the submissive humiliation of her position was only adding, bit by bit, to the explosive orgasm she'd been denied earlier.

It wasn't the worst thing in the world.

By the time Jackson came back, she was so wet that she could feel the moisture dripping down her thighs.

"Get up," he said from somewhere behind her.

Slowly Ava pushed herself off the counter, stiffer than she would have thought. The movement shifted the vibe inside her, and she clenched around it, sending another shudder rippling through her body. She turned to find him smiling, with a large duffel bag over his shoulder and leather gloves on his hands. He was wearing a thick fleece.

He picked up the receiver to speak to the front desk again. Clive. He'd made arrangements through Clive. Did Clive know about…?

"Everything ready?" Jackson said into the phone, his eyes resting hungrily on Ava's naked breasts. "Good. Thank you. Much appreciated, believe me. Look for that envelope at the desk tomorrow."

He hung up the phone, never once taking his eyes off her nakedness. His mouth tightened into a grim line, and he took a deep breath.

"Not yet, Reed," he said to himself. "Ava, put your boots on."

Ava gave him a perplexed expression. She was naked; she wasn't—

"And only your boots."

Slowly it began to dawn on her. His clothes. His gloves. Her boots.

"*Now*, Ava."

chapter 17

Getting the boots on had been harder than Ava had expected with the red anal vibe still inside her. It didn't seem like it was about to fall out of her, but the fear that it would kept her clenched tight. And Jackson had made sure to tell her to keep it in. He hadn't helped. He'd just watched her, his eyes gleaming.

She still couldn't quite believe what was about to happen. She didn't know, not exactly, but it seemed pretty likely that it would involve being outside.

She risked a look over her shoulder. It was still snowing, the flakes coming down big and heavy.

"Ava," Jackson said sharply.

She snapped back around at full attention.

"You're going to follow me. Keep the vibe in. You'll find walking a little strange at first," he said, a smile playing at his lips. "But you'll get used to it."

"Follow you?" she said.

"Anything you don't understand about that?"

"I just...don't..."

"You are going to follow me, naked, and with that red vibe sticking out of your ass, into the hallway, where, yes, I suppose any of my neighbors could come out into the hall and see you," he said evenly. "And you are going to do it *now*."

That voice.

Meekly, she nodded. He opened the door for her, his ingrained chivalry almost making her laugh under the circumstances. It was perfect, it really was. That was who he was.

But then there was the hallway. Cold and gleaming, the modern lines of the place designed to make everything look expensive and smooth. She took her first steps, paying careful attention to the way the vibe moved inside her. He was right; she could already tell the sensations would build and build, like they had when she'd stayed bent over the counter.

She could feel the folds of her labia sliding together as she walked past him. He took a deep breath.

Oh God, can he smell me?

The thought made her feel wanton, and easy, like he could get her to do anything and everything. *He probably can.*

There. She was standing naked in the hallway of a luxury apartment building. And it did heighten everything, like some kind of insane drug. If he touched her.... But Jackson only stood in the open doorway for a moment, taking in the sight of her, standing there, shaking slightly, her nipples pebbling at the sheer excitement of it.

He followed after her without a word, letting the door close behind them, and then turned down the hall. She followed, walking quickly to make up for the short little strides demanded by the vibe.

Jackson walked past the elevator, and she could have died from the relief. So not the elevator, at least. But where?

The stairway. Of course. He already had the door open, and she sped up, hurrying for the relative privacy of the stairwell. She thought she heard him chuckle as she shimmied past him into the fluorescent gloom. The door clanged behind them with finality.

Ava hugged her arms to her chest and shivered. There was a certain chill in the stairwell. Jackson was on the top floor. The roof was just above and…the door was open. The door to the roof.

Ava looked back at Jackson in disbelief. He smiled.

Jackson slung the duffel bag around, unzipped it, and extracted a thick, warm looking blanket. "Wrap this around yourself," he instructed. "It's designed for arctic expeditions. Very warm."

Dutifully, she wrapped herself in the soft blanket. He was right. He was always right. Already the chill was gone. But…the roof?

"Jackson…"

"Get up those stairs, Ava," he said. "Now."

She was startled, and found that her feet were moving, almost of their own accord, one in front of the other, step by step. It was that voice—that voice that was like a psychic leash, leading her around while she was in this state. She was moving inexorably toward the roof. Toward whatever he had planned. And she liked it.

The roof was beautiful in the snow, in a way that was unique to New York. The maintenance sheds and vents and various other functional things that took up part of any large rooftop created their own topography, giving rise to wind currents and eddies, visible only because of the falling snow. And below was Manhattan, the snow cover lit up by the life of the city.

"Over here," Jackson ordered, pointing to an area near the edge where the snow hadn't accumulated. Ava felt it as soon as she stepped in: warm gusts of air billowing out around her blanket. This was the part of the roof where the heating vents were. And there was some kind of apparatus constructed out of sturdy looking pipes and beams, something that rose above her head and extended out to the edge of the roof.

"You are a freaking lunatic," she said, almost dazed.

"I'm going to pretend I didn't hear that," he said, laughing. She couldn't see his face in the dark. "Give me the blanket."

The air from the vents cut the ice from the wind, but it wasn't exactly warm. She shivered, and she felt her whole body contract. The wetness on her thighs was cold now. But she obeyed, and gave him the blanket. She watched him fold it carefully and place it in the duffel while retrieving something else she couldn't quite make out. It was surreal to be standing in the middle of falling snow, chilly but not freezing, and *naked*.

Jackson moved under the main beam of the contraption that rose above them and said, "Come here."

She couldn't help but look up as she did. The grey sky and the falling snow hid any details of the appartus.

"Look at me," he said.

She did. His eyes were steady, and burned with that look she'd come to know. There was a beat where they only looked at each other, and everything seemed to pass between them—what she'd asked him for, what he'd promised her—and then he tied a blindfold around her eyes.

Ava felt the beginnings of a panic response. She flushed with heat, and her lungs gasped for air. She reached out blindly, clawing at the empty space, filled with terror at finding nothing, and then he was there. He caught her hands and brought them to his chest, wrapping his arms around her.

"Not going anywhere," he said gruffly, and held her so tight that she could hardly breathe. Somehow it calmed her. She vastly preferred this feeling to the horror of being suddenly alone.

He stroked her hair. "That's better," he said.

She sighed into his chest, feeling sleepy until he spanked her right over the vibe. It sent a jolt right through to her clit, and she took a sharp breath. She couldn't help but rub her nipples ever so slightly against his sweater. She felt the chuckle deep in his chest more than heard it before he stepped away.

"Put out your arms and spread your legs," he ordered.

Ava did as he asked immediately, not questioning or wondering. She found she wasn't surprised to feel soft ropes sliding over her skin, or at the feel of leather wrapped around her waist, thighs, and ankles, or the sounds of latches and buckles. With each knot he tied, she surrendered a little more of herself, let one more psychological bind unravel. It felt like finally taking off uncomfortable clothing at the end of a long day, only…so much more so.

Finally, he was done. She didn't know what she looked like, but the ropes were cutting into the skin around her ribcage and breasts, and she could feel them already starting to swell. As if he was reading her thoughts, Jackson grasped her breasts and pinched both of her nipples, hard.

"Oh God, Jackson," she said. Her knees buckled. Her nipples were sensitive, swollen, and raw. Her clit was throbbing, and the vibe in her ass was demanding that she get some relief—soon. "Please," she said.

"Turn around."

He grabbed her arms and pulled them behind her and bound them there. It was a little uncomfortable, and it thrust her back out and her chest up.

And then the ropes started to pull.

She was lifted from the seat first, and she realized he must have her in some kind of harness. But she was pulled from multiple points until she was lifted into the air, totally unable to move on her own. The lines attached to her lower half pulled tighter, raising her legs and her bottom until she felt like her head must be angled toward the ground. And then the lines attached to her ankles began to pull in opposite directions, spreading her legs. They pulled, and kept pulling, until she thought she would split.

When it all finally stopped, she was blindfolded, suspended in the air, bottom angled up, arms bound behind her, and legs spread wide. She was panting for breath.

"Remember not to come," he said, and then there were hands on her buttocks, pulling her slightly forward, and a warm, wet mouth on her pussy.

"Oh my God," she screamed. She tried to writhe, to pull away, because she was sure she would come at any instant, but she was bound and helpless, and he ignored her. It was like he needed to drink his fill, and he lapped at her mercilessly, fucking her with his tongue while pressing on the protruding vibe. Briefly, he took her clit between his teeth, then wrapped his lips around it and sucked cruelly. She almost cried before her let her go, setting her swinging gently in the air.

"Almost," he said. He sounded hoarse.

Ava heard him move slightly away, and then there was the sound of the pulleys again, and she felt herself begin to move laterally, parallel with the ground. Still blindfolded, it took her a moment to orient herself, but eventually she was certain: she was moving towards the edge of the roof.

"Jackson," she said. She was still moving. The sounds of the city below were getting louder. When she finally stopped, she felt herself swaying in the air, and she didn't stop until he put his hand on her lower belly to steady her.

"Almost," he said again.

He pressed down on the base of the vibe that

was still in her ass, and it started to softly vibrate. Ava moaned. She could feel those vibrations in her clit, in her nipples, in her fingertips, in her freaking teeth.

"Don't you come," he said, and as though to test her obedience, he began to rotate the vibe inside of her. She had grown so accustomed to it that it didn't hurt at all, and now she could feel herself stretching, opening, inviting.

"That's right," he said, and more cold lube fell on her. "I'm going to take your ass."

Something pulled on her blindfold and it fell away. Ava gasped and had to keep herself from screaming. She was looking over Manhattan, hanging off the edge of the roof, suspended in the air and spread for Jackson's pleasure.

"Oh, holy shit!" she cried. "Oh God, oh God, oh God…"

She'd known it was coming as soon as he'd led her up here—of course she had—but that knowledge was nothing to the actual sight, the experience. She was babbling, mumbling over and over, her chest heaving against the ropes and her core alight, when Jackson removed the vibe. Immediately, it was replaced with the tip of something else, something warm, something much, much bigger.

"Jackson," she said.

"Trust me," he said. And grabbed her hips with both hands, swinging her whole body onto his rigid cock, and pushed himself slowly inside her.

She lifted her head as much as she could, shaking, sure she couldn't take him. He felt her strain, looked up sharply, and said, "Relax. Let it wash over you."

That voice. She let her head drop, watched the city below her, the skyline inverted from her nearly upside down position, and did just that, no matter how ridiculous it was. She relaxed into the ropes, into herself, into Jackson. She felt completely supported and left with no choice but to submit. It was like she was floating, like the world spun gently around them both, and she felt like finally, finally, when held up like this, she could let go.

The pressure increased, and she felt that same pop as he forced the head of his cock into her. Slowly, he guided her fully onto him until she was impaled on his dick.

"So tight," he groaned. He pulled out slightly, holding her in place with his hands, and gently pushed into her again. Her whole body began to sway as he rocked slowly with his hips, one hand still guiding her, the other pressing into her lower belly, his thumb rubbing against her clit.

The pressure inside her was intense. She kept blinking, looking out as snow fell around her, and water shed from her eyes, though she wasn't crying. The moisture that fell to the sides of her face reminded her of how cold it was outside. She should have been freezing, but the warmth of the vents and the feeling that had begun to pulsate out from her core overwhelmed any other concerns.

"Please," she managed. Somehow, it was hard to talk. All she knew was that she ached to feel even fuller.

The rocking stopped, and she heard the familiar sound of the duffel. He must have hung it nearby, and soon she knew why. More lube, and then the feel of that blue rubber vibe poised at the entrance to her vagina.

"Oh God," she moaned.

Slowly he pulled partway out of her ass as he pushed the vibe into her pussy. He alternated the strokes, going deeper each time, until finally she was completely full of both. Words seemed so far away from anything she was capable of, but she managed to cry out, "Jackson!"

Just before he turned the vibrator on.

"Now you will come, Ava," he said. "And don't stop."

Ava wailed into the night as Jackson fucked her slowly and thoroughly with his cock and the vibrator, every nerve in her body lit up and sparkling and telling her to come right fucking now. Her whole body felt like one contracting muscle, like an imploding star, until everything exploded outwards in a rippling wave and vanished.

chapter 18

Jackson dreamt of Ava, and of being interrupted. He dreamt about making love to her, and he dreamt about the moment when she'd said she loved him, only to have something pull him away at the last second.

He awoke to the incessant buzzing of his phone, vibrating its way across a bedside table, but he didn't reach for it. He didn't move for what seemed like a long time. He wanted to get things straight in his mind.

Had it really happened?

Ava had called him. She had needed him, had been upset for some reason that she still hadn't told him about. She had asked him to show her what it felt like to trust someone, and he'd known exactly what she'd meant. Knew she still needed to experience things physically, first. And he'd shown her. Christ, had he shown her.

And then, as he was carrying her to bed, she'd said it almost too softly to hear: *I love you*.

She was there, in his bed now, sleeping soundly next to him. It had all happened.

The joy that gripped his heart hit him so strongly that it almost hurt. For a minute, he couldn't breathe, his chest constricted. She had said it. He reached over to her and she turned onto her side, murmuring a bit. Then she sighed and slipped deeper back into sleep.

Ava's face was peaceful and content. She was the most beautiful woman he'd ever known, and she'd never looked more beautiful than when she was happy.

He doubted she'd slept so well in ages. She looked so goddamn right, lying there in his bed, it made his heart hurt all over again. Jackson was so full of relief and happiness he didn't know where to put it; he turned away, to his phone, just to give himself something else to do. Looking at her like this was like looking at the sun. He'd have to take it in small doses at first.

His fucking phone. Lillian. About a million missed calls and texts to scroll through. No details; Lillian was cautious about that, like he'd told her to be. One phone gets stolen or hacked, and they'd read about the details of their new product on the internet the next day.

But something was obviously wrong.

Fuck. Fuck, fuck, fuck.

Jackson was an engineer by nature. He designed his company to run right, to run with redundancies in place, to run modularly, with the right people heading up the right tasks, people who were good at their jobs and could handle their responsibilities without having to bring the knuckleheaded stuff to his desk. This was one of the reasons he could, if he felt like it, take a couple of days off to thoroughly fuck the love of his life until she agreed to stick around.

But bad design led to chaotic, shoddy, and sometimes catastrophic results. Bad design pissed him off. It meant someone was careless, or lazy, or just bad at their job, and if something was wrong with this product launch—something big enough for his phone to blow up for twenty straight minutes—then that someone was him. It meant he'd lost control of the process.

And it meant he had to leave Ava.

In the end, he just couldn't bring himself to wake her. He tried, gently, but she was sleeping deeply, and Lord knew she needed the rest after the night they'd had. Instead, he made a compromise with himself: the office was ten minutes away, and he swore he'd be back in an hour. And he swore he'd make up every missing minute to her.

He left her an apologetic note on his pillow, dressed hurriedly, and left.

~ ~ ~

The thought—the memory—of Ava saying that she loved him put a smile on Jackson's normally impassive face all the way to the ArTech office. It had been dumb to think he'd be able to think about anything else. She'd said it. All he'd had to do was engineer a meeting, convince her to let him be her temporary sexual fantasy, take her to a private estate, and then suspend her off the roof of his building, but the important thing was: she'd said it.

So what was this little bit of worry that nagged at him?

He barely registered all the other young twenty-somethings who worked for the various start-ups and media companies that rented space in this building. There was a well put together little blonde, hair in an artfully messed bun, first button of her button-down open, who tried to give him a smile in the elevator. Mostly he noticed that she was not Ava.

He wondered if Ava was still asleep. He hoped so; she had gone out like a light. He grimaced at the thought of her waking up without him after what she'd said. The elevator was stopping at every damn floor on the way up for people to go to and from their coffee and cigarette breaks, and every unnecessary delay annoyed the shit out of him on this particular morning. The doors opened yet again, and two goateed and soul-patched graphic design looking types, coats on and cigarettes already out, got on, not minding the ride to the top.

Fantastic.

Goatee number one rubbed his eyes. "Man, I don't even remember last night."

The phrase tore through Jackson. *Don't even remember last night.* Ava had been deep in subspace; she'd only barely come out long enough for him to check in with her before she fell asleep. It was entirely possible that she wouldn't remember what she'd said. Or that she'd think it had been a dream.

Or that she wouldn't be sure.

Furious with himself, Jackson jabbed viciously at the '14' button.

"Whoa, man. Chill out," said Goatee number two.

Jackson turned to face them. He took a moment to look them up and down. Finally he said, "I advise you very seriously to mind your own fucking business. Is that clear?"

The two goatees mumbled something and turned to face forward. Jackson knew he'd regret the outburst later; losing control in any facet of his life wasn't acceptable to him. But damn it, *Ava.* And now he'd been torn away by some apparently unmanageable crisis at his company, the place he'd painstakingly built over the last decade, the thing he'd lived and breathed until Ava had come back into his life.

Whatever it was had to be bad. Lillian wouldn't waste his time on the stupid stuff.

"Come *on*," Jackson muttered as the doors closed on twelve.

It was just before the doors opened on 14, ArTech's floor, that Jackson realized there was something even worse than Ava not remembering: Ava remembering.

And freaking the hell out.

"Fuck!" Jackson said, and pushed his way through the barely open doors, immediately in search of Lillian. Whatever it was, whatever the giant freaking crisis was, he'd damn well better find a way to deal with it within the hour and get back to the woman who made him absolutely insane. Ava's well documented history of running away from anything approaching closeness, or anytime it looked like she might get hurt—like if the guy she'd just confessed her love to fucking *vanished* the next morning—gave him more than enough reason for concern. The idea of her waking up under those circumstances, with him gone, caused an actual physical pain in his chest.

Christ, that's why they call it heartache.

He'd never forgive himself for being so monumentally stupid. Never. Whatever was wrong with ArtLingua had better be worth his time. He found Lillian off in a corner.

"Lillian," he said tersely, taking her elbow and pulling her out of a group of programmers.

"Jackson, you made it in." He looked at her. Her voice was slightly sarcastic, but she looked as impeccable as always. Maybe a touch more make up, but softer. There was something about her posture, too, something he hadn't seen in her in a while. She went on, "What happened to your coat? You look like a ski bum."

I don't have time for this.

"What the hell is the emergency, Lillian?"

She smiled brilliantly. "I have something to show you." And she walked briskly towards her office.

Something to show me?

Jackson wasn't in the habit of second guessing his COO. It would've defeated the purpose of hiring top-tier talent like Lillian, and insulted her skills, besides. So the feeling that gathered in his gut, that told him this was about to be a giant clusterfuck, was both unfamiliar and unwelcome.

Lillian punched in her personal security code

and unlocked her office door. She gave him a wicked smile over her shoulder and opened the door.

"See anything unusual?" she asked.

Her office was full of canvases. Beautiful canvases, canvases with some of the most provocative art from the most recent gallery shows. Stuff he had personally scouted out and brought into the conversations about ArtLingua. Stuff that was all on the verge of busting out big, but hadn't quite yet. The biggest, most impressive piece — the one that dominated every room he'd ever seen it in, including this one — was leaning up against the far wall. It was a kind of controlled explosion of reds and blacks and various mixed media, all of it coming together until you realized it was a crowd, a sea of humanity. It was by a guy named Moreau out of Detroit, and it was Jackson's second favorite painting. His first favorite was still hidden in the back of his closet at home.

Where Ava was.

"What am I looking at, Lil?" he asked quietly. One thing Jackson was certain of: this did not add up to a crisis.

"I asked Arlene — you know she's dating the owner of the Borsa Gallery?"

"Yes. Get to the point. What's the problem?"

Lillian looked at him. She finally seemed to be catching on to the fact that he was in no mood.

"We've acquired all of these, on loan, for the ArtLingua launch party. We'll have them set up next to demonstrations of the functionalities they inspired. And this," she said, pointing to the big red and black Moreau, "will be the centerpiece. I wanted to show you in person."

Jackson felt all emotion drain away from him, the way it did before it was replaced by a cold anger. Lillian didn't look confused that he thought there had been something wrong. She looked satisfied. She wasn't a woman who made mistakes.

"This is why you called me in?" he asked quietly. "There was no emergency? No problem with the launch?"

"Oh, no," she said, waving her hand like it was nothing. "I was just excited. I thought you'd be in, actually. I saw that your companion left separately this past weekend, and I just assumed... Why? Is everything ok?"

Jackson closed his eyes. He couldn't believe he used to think of Lillian's constant, manipulative games as entertaining. He had looked at is as jousting, the kind of thing where it was satisfying to gain the upper hand. It had never really suited him, but he'd had to try it to find out for sure.

"Arlene's been working on this for months," he finally said. "This isn't new. You know I came here thinking there was some kind of emergency, Lillian, and you know it because you deliberately gave me that impression. Don't give me any bullshit. And don't call me again unless there's an actual goddamned reason."

She opened her mouth to speak, but one look at Jackson's face made her think better of it. Jackson stood still for another beat until he was sure he had control of himself. He had a plan. That plan was to get back to Ava and make sure things hadn't gotten royally screwed up. A terrible feeling had descended upon him, one he recognized from the depths of the childhood he tried not to think about, and that feeling was dread.

Wordlessly, he turned around and headed back toward Ava.

After that, Jackson's self control was tested mightily. He hopped in a cab, determined to get home as fast as possible, and the cab proceeded to hit every possible type of traffic. Roadwork, a delayed delivery truck, a branch down on some power lines from the weight of the ice. By the time he decided to run the rest of the way, cursing when he stepped in a slush puddle as he jumped out of the cab, he really had been gone for an hour. At least.

Don't get worked up, Reed. It's probably nothing.

He managed to calm himself with that thought in the elevator ride up. Right up until he opened the door to his empty apartment.

Ava was gone.

chapter 19

The first time Ava had woken up, warm and safe and cradled in Jackson's arms, she couldn't quite believe what had happened. Any of it. Not that she'd run to his apartment, finally driven by fear and desperation and sense that she deserved a shot, and demanded that he...what? That he show her what he had to offer. And holy crap, he had. If it weren't for the persistent but pleasant aches of various parts of her body, she'd be convinced that what had happened on the roof must have been a dream.

But no, it had been real. The strangest part for Ava was that when she woke up in the middle of the night with a sleeping Jackson wrapped around her, hours after the roof, hours after he'd carried her back to bed and talked her down, hours after they'd fallen asleep together, she still felt the same. Open. Safe. Strong.

Maybe this thing will stick, was the last thing she

thought as she fell back asleep.

When she woke again in the morning, however, Jackson was gone. There was only a note: *Emergency at work. I'll be back in an hour.*

The most extraordinary part of this whole experience—waking up alone after such an intense night, finding a very brief note—was how much it didn't bother her. Or rather, didn't panic her. Didn't immediately play on her insecurities, or trigger all of her myriad defenses. It wasn't ideal, but Ava was sure there had been an emergency, and at some point it became unrealistic that a CEO would be able to just play hooky indefinitely.

Those were all things she would have always known rationally, but actually feeling calm was pretty new to her.

She liked it.

And it gave her plenty of time to settle in and sort herself out. The events of the past week were of the life-changing variety, and she had to make sense of what those changes were.

Her mother was getting married. Her mother was sober. Ellie seemed happy. Ava couldn't seem to care about her job, which, if she didn't call in soon with some incredible news, she might very well lose. And then there was Jackson...

Then there was Jackson.

She tried to imagine her reaction to her mother's announcement if she hadn't spent all that time with Jackson, if she'd never taken him up on his offer. On her debt. He kept saying she owed him the opportunity to repay her, or something like that, but she'd never gotten an explanation out of him. She hadn't had time. She'd been...distracted.

There was no way she would even be contemplating calling her mother to offer her congratulations—and an apology—if it hadn't been for Jackson. None—no chance in hell. Obviously, she hadn't yet; there were some things that were never going to be easy. But she was thinking about it.

All of these emotions and thoughts and new, frightening ways of looking at things swirled around inside her, brewing up a tempest, until Ava was left with only one stable desire at the furious eye of the storm: she needed to paint.

It was the only way she was going to see things clearly. She hadn't felt the need to paint like this in…God, she couldn't remember. But the only time in her life she'd ever felt anything like the way she had while surrendering such control, filled with peace, had been when she was painting.

Ava smiled to herself. She'd only felt full of peace for part of the time on the roof. The rest had been of a different nature. She'd never managed to paint *that* kind of picture, but with Jackson as inspiration, anything was possible.

Ava froze. *Inspiration.* That was it. That was undoubtedly, profoundly, wretchedly it. He had inspired her in every possible way. He was still…

Oh God, I said it.

She was alone, but Ava covered her eyes with one hand anyway. No, she was sure. She had absolutely, one hundred percent, told Jackson Reed that she loved him. While curled up against his chest and blissed out beyond all belief on the things he'd done to her, granted, but she had still said it. She had meant it, she had been past the point of keeping stuff like that to herself, and she had said the actual human words, in English, out loud.

"Oh, fuck me," she said to an empty room.

Ava knew just what she had to do. She scribbled her own terse note on the back of the one Jackson had left, and got dressed.

~ ~ ~

Ava's crappy apartment building felt both familiar and totally foreign. It simply wasn't the same after the past few days, and it was hard not to see it with new eyes. She picked her way over the iced-over sidewalks, not surprised in the least that no one had bothered to properly salt the sidewalks in front of the buildings like they were supposed to. It was dangerous, no doubt about it, and just one more piece of evidence that she lived in the only horrible old tenement building that the developers hadn't gotten to yet. It was probably inevitable that it would become another set of luxury condos, not all that different from the one Jackson lived in, if considerably less expensive. The slum-lord who owned her building was probably just waiting for the zoning commission or a bidding war or one of the many other scenarios made possible by the city's arcane real estate laws.

Yet this was where Ava chose to live, just so she could have a two-bedroom. Just so she could have a room to paint in. *That probably should have clued me in*, she thought as she gingerly made her way up the frozen stoop. She stopped to say hi to Jim, the homeless guy who hung out over the heating grate in front of her building. She dropped some change in his cup and waved.

"You have anywhere to go if it gets really bad?" she asked. "They say this cold snap's going to last another night."

"I got a place," he said, blowing into his hands. "Unlocked boiler room. Don't you worry about me."

Ava didn't push it. Jim was famously resistant to what he called "being tied down." Ava didn't know much about the guy except that he'd obviously had bad experiences with state services, and he seemed to take responsibility for making sure no one hassled the residents of her building, which she appreciated. Heroin deals were kept to the park a couple of blocks away, at least. He was like the poor man's doorman. She asked him, "New coat?"

Jim smiled. "Nice, ain't it?"

"Keep warm," she said, and pushed her way into the building, dismayed to find that the locks on the building door still hadn't been fixed. There had been a wave of push-in robberies in the neighborhood over the past few months, and there was nothing more terrifying to a single woman living in the city than the phrase "push-in," when someone pushed open your door and forced their way in. It was probably foolish to take comfort in the fact that Jim kept his post downstairs, but it was what she had. She made a mental note to have new deadbolts put in on her apartment door, landlord be damned, and thought hard about the cherished studio she was there to see.

The hallway was unheated, and Ava hurried up

the three flights of stairs to her apartment, where she'd at least be able to turn the radiator on full blast. When she'd first moved into this place, she'd taken a silly kind of pride in the gritty romanticism of artistic New York poverty. Now it just seemed cold and uncomfortable.

But she did have her studio. And she wouldn't need the heat for what she had planned, anyway.

She let herself in and looked around as she slowly unwound herself from all her winter gear. Her apartment didn't really feel like home. It felt like a temporary sublet. She'd never properly decorated or put much effort into making it hers. Except, of course, for the second bedroom, where she painted.

In there, it was a riot of messy, unrestrained color, paints and canvases all over the place. Ages ago, she'd strung up sheets on all the walls and taped them carefully around the one window so she didn't have to worry about getting paint everywhere, and then she'd taken full advantage of that security. It looked like she'd had a constant paint party for the past few years. She couldn't help but laugh; it was like she had her own playroom.

And I've been terrified to let anyone even know it exists.

Ava wanted to roll her eyes at her own foolishness, but she still felt too raw. Even now, standing in the middle of all of it, she could still feel that familiar anxiety start to come back. Some things wouldn't change overnight. But she'd come here with a purpose, with the kind of sudden inspiration that she knew to trust, and just because she was starting to get cold feet didn't mean she could chicken out.

Or run away.

She was definitely determined not to run away ever again. She wouldn't do that to Jackson, or to herself.

Jackson, who'd already given her so, so much. Ava looked around at her most recent paintings, the ones she'd done just prior to Jackson's sudden reappearance in her life. They were troubling, but not totally surprising. Lots of splitting, as she thought of it, diametrically opposed color choices, split compositions. And a general sense of claustrophobia, of the world weighing in, of being trapped. They were actually pretty good, but not if you were the person who had painted them. Not if you wanted to be happy.

Holy crap, am I happy?

Ava did the mental equivalent of patting herself down. In the absence of any other evidence, she was going to have to say…yeah. Maybe.

Whoa. How did that happen?

She supposed the pictures told part of the story. The first half, anyway. Ava hadn't always painted like this. She used to do portraits. Those portraits were always her little love letters to the people she painted, and to the world at large. They were her fervent attempts to capture the best things she saw in people, and for a while, they'd helped her to feel close and connected to the world around her. But they were also very intensely personal. Ava didn't know if it was possible to paint the way she wanted to and not reveal so much of herself to the world, but if it was, she hadn't figured it out, and she was pretty sure she didn't want to. That was the promise of those paintings: real connection.

So, of course, she'd stopped showing them to people. And then she'd stopped painting them entirely.

But then Jackson had happened.

And now I'm going to start again.

Ava turned on the old, paint-splattered boom box that was her constant painting companion, turned up the equally old Bjork CD she had in there, and started to gather her materials. She was just getting into the groove when she heard the door smash in.

chapter 20

Jackson ran through his apartment, trying to fend off the worst of his thoughts, opening every door, looking insanely in closets and bathrooms, but then he'd seen the note he'd left on the floor on his side of the bed, and he'd realized she probably hadn't seen it. Not that it necessarily would have made a difference, if she were freaking out over having told him she loved him. But he might have felt less guilty.

No. There was nothing that was going to make him feel better—not now. Ava Barnett had run away from him again. He had lost her. Again.

"No," he said aloud in his now lonely apartment. "Fucking...*no*."

This was not happening again. It couldn't.

Jaw clenched tight, he methodically called her cell phone. He'd only recently gotten the number, as though that made any goddamn sense. *Yes*, he thought viciously, *I'll trust you to tie me up and fuck me, but giving you my phone number is a big step.*

Carefully, he cooled his anger while the phone rang. He didn't want to be angry with her. He didn't want her to pick up the phone and have the first thing she heard be anger. He knew that wasn't right.

He needn't have worried. She didn't pick up. Not the first time he called, not the third, not the fifth.

He collapsed to the floor, hands covering his head. This couldn't be what it looked like. She wouldn't do this again.

"Fucking *bullshit!*" he shouted.

He knew where she lived. She could at least actually tell him she didn't want to see him again. He at least deserved that.

~ ~ ~

Jackson actually jogged across town, slowing down only where the ice demanded it, and made it to Alphabet City in just under fifteen minutes. He barely felt it, even without a proper warm up. He hadn't felt adrenaline like this since football. But then, football had never carried with it this sense of impending disaster.

Stop it, Reed. Just find your girl.

He recognized her building right away. It looked even worse in the light of day. He didn't want her living like this, even if she never wanted to see him again, not that he'd have any say in it. Christ, it didn't look even remotely safe. There were obvious drug dealers hanging around in the park on the next block—heroin, if he remembered his tabloid headlines correctly. And where there were addicts, there were robberies.

Glowering and breathing hard, his shoulders bunching up in his old ski jacket and his hands curling into fists, he approached the stoop. Jackson did a double take when he recognized his old coat on the man sitting on the heating grate.

"Hey," the man said, making the effort to get up. "It's you. The coat man."

"It do the job?" Jackson said, catching his breath. He noted the names on the buzzers. 3A, Barnett. He pressed the buzzer, but it didn't appear to work.

"Yessir. What're you doing back here? Thought you got lucky."

Jackson choked on a laugh, even though it wasn't funny. Not in the least. The homeless guy brushed some straggly hair out of his eyes and studied him.

"Well," Jackson finally said, his chest starting to hurt from the run. "Not as lucky as I thought. Trying to fix that. I'm here to see a woman."

"Well, go on in. Door's unlocked. I know you're good people."

Jackson stared at him. The homeless guy waved him on, like Jackson had passed a test, and went back to his seat on the heating grate. Jackson pushed on the door, and lo and behold, it just opened. In this neighborhood.

Fantastic.

The fear that Ava had left him for good intensified, spiked with the new fear he felt for her safety. It was a strong mix.

He took the stairs two at a time, glad to keep

moving since the hallway wasn't heated, but he couldn't get ahead of it. Couldn't get ahead of the feeling. It was creeping up on him, making him madder and madder.

He raced across the landing on the second floor, trying to outrun it.

His mind was full of warring, terrible thoughts: on the one hand, Ava in trouble, unsafe in this shitty building, this shitty neighborhood. On the other, Ava not caring, just leaving him again, like he was worthless. Neither of them fit the image he had of Ava, but nothing made sense to him at all, with her gone.

Jackson reached the door marked 3A, breathing hard from the run, the stairs, and the need to see her right fucking now. He could hear music from inside. Music. He pounded on the door, calling out her name, but there was nothing. No response. Like he didn't even exist.

"Ava!" he shouted.

He had hold of the doorknob in his big hand and he rattled the thin door with every blow of his fist. How could she not hear him?

"GodDAMN it!" he yelled, and threw himself against the door.

No one was more surprised than him when it gave way.

Jackson stood in the middle of a modest, messy living room, looking big and dumb, and with an aching shoulder. The door swung uselessly behind him. He was suddenly aware that he had just broken into Ava's apartment.

"I didn't mean to," he said out loud to no one at all. He was alone in the strangely lonely looking living room.

As if that fucking matters.

The quick remorse of a little kid who'd been roughhousing too hard passed through him momentarily. The music was coming from a bedroom.

What the hell was going on?

He couldn't quite bring himself to believe that he'd find her in there with another man, but he'd also just told himself she would be at his home, waiting for him, he'd also just told himself everything would work out, and he very clearly didn't know what the fuck he was talking about when it came to Ava Barnett. He took two giant, seething strides towards the door with the music behind it, and shoved it open.

And got hit in the face by a flying boom box.

It didn't hurt him so much as stun him. It hit him square on the nose, and for a moment, he could see nothing. In the next second, someone tried to run past them, and he instinctively grabbed them and held on. He only wanted to make everything stop until he had a handle on what was happening, until everything slowed down and decided to make sense. Several things penetrated his adrenaline-soaked brain in a slow, terrible progression: whoever was struggling under him now was much smaller than him; whoever was struggling under him was afraid; and whoever was struggling under him was screaming his name.

There were certain evolutionarily determined consequences to getting unexpectedly hit in the face, particularly for someone who wasn't used to it. One of them was the panic blindness. Acting without thinking. But eventually those blinders fell away, and Jackson Reed was stunned to find himself holding a screaming, crying Ava Barnett as though she were some kind of threat to him.

He let her go.

She backed as far away from him as she could get, which, since he still stood in the doorway, was back into the room she'd come from. Not good. Jackson still didn't understand everything that was going on around him—there were sheets on the walls? It looked like a padded cell—but then his eyes fell on Ava, and everything else vanished.

She was crying. She was shaking. He had done that.

He wanted to die.

"Ava," he began.

"What the fuck are you doing?" she said, very quietly. "I thought... There have been push-ins around here. I thought you were..."

Jackson touched his face and his fingers came away red. His nose was bleeding. It was pretty clear what she'd thought was happening, and he couldn't imagine what that did to a woman, in particular. This might be the most frightening experience of her life. He had done that. She was crouched in the far corner of the room, between rows of canvases, clutching a paintbrush. She was still shaking.

Otherwise, things had gotten very still. It felt very dangerous. A part of him that was detached noted the irony: now he felt in danger. A moment ago, he'd made Ava feel that way. The rest of him was in full-blown 'holy shit I fucked up and I don't even know how it happened' mode.

"I thought you'd left," he said. It sounded so stupid when he said it like that.

"What?" she said. She seemed confused. "I did leave. I left you a note. I was coming back."

"No, I thought…"

Oh fuck, she left me a note. As if it fucking mattered. As if anything would undo what he had done.

"I thought you'd left. For real. Permanently." It didn't sound any better when he said it out loud. Jackson was stuck with the fact that he'd done something terrible.

"What are you doing here?" he asked her, miserable.

"Me? What am I doing here? I *live* here, you fucking psycho!" She threw the paintbrush at him. It was loaded with paint, scarlet red. It left an indelible mark on his dressed down suit. "What the fuck are you doing breaking into my apartment?"

"It was an accident."

Ava stared at him. "Exactly how do you break into an apartment *accidentally*?"

She didn't wait for an answer. Instead, she began to pace in the small room, walking in and out of the thin light from the window. Watery winter light bounced off of her hair as she shook her hands violently, like she needed to work off the energy, the shakes. Jackson recognized that. It wasn't a good feeling.

He would have to explain. He didn't know if he could explain, even to himself. "I just…I came here because I thought you'd left. I thought you'd left me — again — that you'd freaked out because…"

"Because?"

Ava had stopped pacing, and now all of her terrible fury was focused on Jackson. As it should be. As was right.

"Because you said you loved me."

Whatever Jackson expected next, he didn't expect Ava Barnett to cry. But she did, in great, big, heaving sobs, slowly collapsing into an unformed ball, and when he tried to come forward to comfort her, she scuttled off into another corner without even thinking, a reflexive action that hurt him to his core. She regarded him as a danger. As a threat. As someone who would barge into…

What was this place?

For the first time, he looked around. And when he processed what he saw, he hated himself even more. It was obviously her studio. A place she came to paint. Canvases everywhere, canvases he would have dreamed of seeing under different circumstances. The place where the real Ava Barnett lived, the most cherished, protected part of herself. And he'd invaded, broken in, violated the only thing she held sacred.

"You told me you didn't paint anymore," he said hollowly.

"I told *Lillian* I didn't paint anymore. You didn't ask," came the reply from the corner.

"Would you have told me?"

She didn't answer. He probably didn't deserve it. He'd never seen anyone so raw in his entire life.

And then he got to watch her reassemble herself, as she'd done so many times before. Only this time, it was because of him. The armor she assembled around herself, piece by miserable piece, in this place that should have been her own—she needed it because of him. Ava rose up slowly, dried her face, straightened her spine. Finally, she turned her head toward him regally.

"I want you to go."

"No," he said. Jackson knew it was wrong, but it was the wrong of a desperate man. "Please?"

Again, she stared at him. Her hands clawed at her sides. Her expression was molten, changing. There was a fair amount of disbelief there, but also anger, and loss, and grief.

She sat down to cry again. She was still working off the shock.

"Don't touch me," she said before he'd even moved. Like she knew he was thinking about it. Of course she knew. They were still connected. And she'd decided she didn't want him near her. "How could you do this?" she said.

"I'm not this guy. This...I know this was wrong."

He came towards her, slowly at first, making careful steps on the sheet-covered floor. He edged his way around the shield she'd built around herself, wary of every edge, every boundary. He watched her slowly begin to open, to turn towards him.

"Can I hold you?" he asked.

She nodded to him, not looking at him. She seemed miserable.

The feel of her against his body after such a fright was something else he hadn't bargained for. He wanted her again, instantly. He could feel the heat rise in her, too, in the way her hands lingered on his arms, the way her breath quickened.

"What happened?" he asked her.

"Nothing happened, until you broke into my apartment and scared the shit out of me," she said, the anger coming back up. She pulled away from him.

"I came here..." she began, walking off to the other side of the room. He missed her already. "It's none of your business why I came here. You fucking asshole."

For a moment, Jackson was blindsided by that. Clearly, he had been a jackass; clearly, he had fucked up. Looking at her now, quietly sad and angry, he thought, *Oh Christ, I've fucked it up for her, too*.

"No," he said, then again, louder, "No, no, no, no."

Jackson moved towards her again, this time plaintively. This couldn't be.

"This isn't how it's supposed to go," he said to no one in particular. Maybe to the universe.

Ava didn't miss a beat. She swiveled her head around and glared at him. "According to what? Your plan? You fucking Svengali?"

Oh no. Don't...

But it was too late. Her eyes had narrowed, and he could see the gears whirling in her head. Ava's gifts of perception seemed mostly tuned to the people outside her immediate circle, like an automatic act of self-preservation—most people didn't really want to know what their closest friends and family really thought or felt all the time—but she could focus those gifts like a laser beam when she wanted to. He could see her running through every encounter, every exchange they'd had. He'd never felt more exposed. It was probably close to the way she felt about him breaking in.

"Was it even chance that you saw me at Stella's engagement party?" she asked finally.

"What?"

"Holy shit, it wasn't! What did you want with me?" Ava's eyes narrowed. "A do-over? So you didn't have to feel like such a dick about something that happened ten years ago? Is that it? Well, get over it. I absolve you. Done. Not such a big deal. You don't have to manipulate and control me to get what you want. You didn't have to put me through this whole... You could have just asked."

"Ava—"

"We're done, right? So get out."

Jackson stood there motionless, not sure what to do. Finally, he said, "That's not it at all. I've set things up a certain way because I care about you, and I've always been really careful about respecting your boundaries. I mean," he added hastily, looking back at the busted door, "I've tried. I've had that in mind."

Ava rolled her head around, like he'd just told her one of those lies that was so blatant that either the liar or the one being lied to must be stupid. "You *tried?* You had it in mind? Jackson, you can't try to control someone and respect their boundaries at the same time. Those things are mutually exclusive, you utter asshole."

He reached for her again, completely out of ideas. She jumped away. "You don't get it. If you try to control someone, Jacks, you don't respect them. And you can't..."

She stopped, her anger suddenly giving way to

tears. She took a moment to fight them back, and when she looked at him again, her blue eyes were cold and clear. "You can't love someone you don't respect."

"You're wrong," he said, the frustration coming back to him. How could she possibly think that? After everything he'd done? "I do respect you. I do love you. Ava, come on. I always have."

"How would I know any of that?" All the fury and tears had gone from her, and what was left was a quiet, calm shell of sadness. This was the most terrifying incarnation yet, he realized, because it looked final. Stable. Settled. His engineer's mind recognized equilibrium when he saw it, but this was an equilibrium that locked him out.

"Seriously, Jackson," she said again. "How would I know any of that? You push me all the time to talk to you, to open up to you, but you don't do the same with me. You don't tell me anything. You mastermind all these...these stunts, but how am I supposed to know if what I feel with you is real and not just wishful thinking if you don't open up to me, too? That it's not just...that I'm not just convenient for you, until something happens and..."

Ava stopped herself, putting her hand to her face, and he was reminded of how much he still didn't know. How much he'd thought she was going to share with him. He had the terrible suspicion that maybe, just maybe, he'd triggered something, something she'd seen before. Something he didn't know about.

"How am I supposed to trust you? And then you do something like this." She motioned sadly at the busted up door in the next room. "I mean, Jackson, this is *nuts*. And I have to wonder at all that stuff I don't know, and if I'm just crazy to ever think of trusting you at all."

Jackson didn't have an answer. Panic that someone he cared about might be hurt or might have left him wasn't new to him; and neither was the fear that he had lost control of himself, that he'd crossed a line. In fact, both of those fears were distressingly familiar, and it hurt him profoundly to know how badly he'd fucked up today. He'd been working on himself for a long time, but it hadn't been long enough. He'd crossed a pretty severe line, and it wasn't ok.

But it had not occurred to him before that there was a disparity between what he craved from Ava and what he was willing to give. And it had never occurred to him that she might want to know the things he didn't tell people about; it was just a given to him that he had to keep them hidden. But now that she pointed it out, it did seem pretty damn obvious.

Jackson was accustomed to seeing all the angles of a given problem before anyone else. The genius wonder boy didn't have much experience in being flat out wrong, or being caught off-guard. He wasn't very good at either.

"But I love you," he said stubbornly.

"I can't see you right now," Ava said. "I don't... Please don't take this the wrong way, Jackson, I'm just...I'm just scared. And I don't mean physically, necessarily, I just...I don't feel safe."

She lowered her eyes, like she knew how badly that would hurt him and didn't want to see it happen. And nothing had ever hurt him like that.

She didn't feel safe.

It felt like someone had scooped out a big part of his insides and now he was slowly collapsing in on the cavity to try to dull the hurt. He wanted to find someone to beat the shit out of him, because it would make him feel better, it would feel right, and he was sure he deserved it. The gaping maw of grief kept getting bigger and bigger the longer he stood in that room, looking at Ava while she wouldn't look at him, until he just couldn't stand it anymore and had to make his unwilling feet move.

"I'm so sorry," he said, and left.

chapter 21

As soon as Jackson stepped off the plane, he felt it. He always felt it when he came back to Cushing, Oklahoma: the past, weighing down on him, clamoring for his attention. He'd begged his mother to move, but only half-heartedly. She had friends there, as well as memories, and now that his father was truly gone—dead, not just on a bender somewhere between security jobs, but dead and gone and not about to bother anyone ever again—he supposed there was nothing for her to worry about.

She did like her cruises, though. Jackson grinned. He was about to send her on another one, this time to the Bahamas. She'd done Alaska in the summer, had sent him about a million pictures of glaciers. It made her so happy, and he liked to see her face when he gave her the tickets. He tried to do that as often as he could, but sometimes he just sent them in the mail, too busy with work to get away from the city.

Now was an especially crazy time to leave New York. The ArtLingua launch party, which they'd set up as a New Year's Eve party, was the hottest ticket in the city, thanks to their publicist, Arlene. Every art star and tech guru in the city would be there, or would try to be. He should be excited. In just one day, he'd be on the verge of the next triumph, another step up on the road to...where, exactly?

That was part of the problem. He'd done what he'd needed to do, proved he could start and run a world-class business. He'd built something he truly believed could help people, a new thing that had not existed before he had conceived of it. And after this launch, he'd be even richer than he already was. He'd be a veritable star.

And he just didn't give a shit. None of it mattered without Ava. He was like a ghost, a shade. Not even half of himself without her. Especially knowing it was his fault, knowing he'd hurt her. Scared her.

Knowing she didn't feel safe.

Jackson had walked around the office on automatic, doing things that needed to be done, even if he didn't really need to be the one to do them. The launch really had gotten to the point of planning where it was out of his hands—he was just micromanaging because he couldn't be at home. She'd only been with him a short time, but already he could feel her everywhere. Could see her everywhere. Christ, he even thought he could smell her. He'd walk into the kitchen to get something to eat, and would remember her bent over the counter and the longing would seize him ferociously, and then be replaced by grief just as quickly. It wrecked him every time. He didn't eat for two days until he finally started ordering out at the office. Even then, he wasn't hungry. He only ate to appease his employees, who were starting to get worried. Jackson Reed was a hollow man.

And that's why he'd come home.

He tried to shake it off on the walk to the rental car, turned the radio up all the way as he drove off. But once he got on those familiar roads, it was just no use. He knew those roads so well he didn't need to think about it, didn't need to occupy his brain, and thoughts of Ava rushed right back into the empty space.

Jackson pulled into the familiar driveway and just sat in the car. He'd come here because he needed help, because he needed to talk to the only person in the world who would understand what he was afraid of, but now he found that he dreaded doing just that. The idea of telling his mother, his own mother, that he'd frightened a woman? That he'd made her feel unsafe? He could barely face the possibility himself. Telling his mother... The thought that she might look at him and have the same fear Jackson did—that she might look at Jackson and see Jackson's father—then he'd know for sure it was true. That right there ranked as his worst nightmare, hands down.

Jackson leaned his miserable head on the steering wheel. Ava had said she couldn't trust him if she didn't know him, couldn't just trust how she felt. Which frustrated him all the more, because he had trusted her just based on that feeling, hadn't he? Based on their connection?

But you didn't trust her enough to tell her about any of this, did you?

The irony was, he kept his past to himself for precisely that reason: he didn't want to frighten people. Especially women. And keeping things from Ava Barnett had had the exact opposite effect.

"I fucking hate irony," Jackson muttered to himself. But there was no use being scared. He'd have to face all this crap. He had just steeled himself and opened the door when he heard the front door creak open.

"Jackson!"

Emmie Reed stood with her baking apron on, flour on her cheek, and her hands on her hips, pretending to be put out at an unannounced visit, but failing to hide her delight at the same time. Jackson gave her the biggest smile he could, and he was genuinely happy to see his mother. He had to brace himself as he watched her limp down the front steps, as he always did, remembering not to wince. Every painful step reproached him for not being able to stop the beating that had caused it.

"Mom," he said, and wrapped his big arms around her.

"Let me go," she laughed. "I've got to roll out this crust before it warms up enough for the gluten to do its thing and ruin it. Come on, come on, let's go!"

Jackson followed behind her dutifully, not having understood most of what she'd said. His mother was a prolific baker, testing out recipes and contributing her own on various cooking websites with a kind of competitive zeal that Jackson admired. She'd get a flinty look in her eye when she was onto something good, and then Jackson would get a package in the mail full of something delicious. It worked out for everyone.

But to get to the kitchen, they had to go through the whole house. Jackson normally went straight to the kitchen door to avoid this. Walking through the old house brought with it the same assault of memories Jackson had felt upon touching down in Cushing, but about a hundred times stronger. He hated it. He'd watched his mother get pushed down those same damn stairs. He *hated* those stairs. Jackson caught himself actually hunching his shoulders, as though readying himself for an attack.

His dad still ruled this place, even from beyond the grave. It didn't seem fair.

He relaxed noticeably when they got to his mother's warm kitchen, the center island cleared off and covered with flour, a big hunk of dough in the middle of it. Emmie Reed didn't waste any time and went right ahead and started working on the dough.

Without even looking up, she said, "Now tell me what the hell happened."

Jackson grinned. He'd gotten his mouth from his mother, that was for sure.

"It's a woman," he said.

His mother looked up, waiting for him to go on. "Of *course* it's a woman, Jackson. None of 'em have ever driven you back here 'til now. What happened?"

He sat on a kitchen stool and sighed. "Ava Barnett."

His mother's eyes sparkled. "I remember that

one."

"Really?"

"Oh yeah. She was the only one you got excited to tell me about. If I recall correctly," Emmie said, looking up from her flattening crust, "you were not actually an item back in the prehistoric era, or whenever it was. I take it that has changed?"

"For about a minute, yeah."

Emmie rolled in silence for a time while Jackson watched her work, replaying the last few days in his head and trying to figure out how to explain it all to his mother. Finally, Emmie lost her patience and rapped the rolling pin on the counter to get his attention.

"Are you gonna tell me or not?"

Just out with it, Jackson.

"I scared her."

Emmie looked at him. "What do you mean you scared her?"

No going back now.

"I mean I got angry, I got scared, because I thought she was leaving me, and I went to her apartment, and…I was wrong. I was all wrong. Mom, I've worked so hard, I've been so scared that I'd be like him, and now…"

Jackson couldn't finish. What else was there to say? He stared down at his hands, the hands that had busted in Ava's door, and experienced a fresh wave of self-loathing.

"Jackson Reed, look at me."

Jackson hadn't been scared like this since he was a boy. And he was scared now that he'd turned into the man who had scared him then. If he saw it in his mother's face, he'd know beyond the shadow of a doubt. He looked up.

His mother said, "What happened? Specifics."

"I was upset. I shoved against her door, and it just—it gave way. It's not an excuse. I broke open her damn door, and scared the crap out of her. And before that I tried to…I don't know, micromanage everything. I was awful, Mom."

His mother had tears in her eyes.

She said, "Listen to me. Of course you have some of him in you. He was your father—it can't be helped. But you are not him. How could you even think that?" She laughed mirthlessly, wiping her eyes with the back of her arm, her hands still covered in flour. "You've made choices to be good, to be kind, to learn how to deal with your temper. You did that all on your own. You're the man you decided to be, Jackson, and I couldn't be prouder of you."

"I didn't do it all on my own," he said quietly. "I had help."

"Well, whatever. You did it. Now what did Ava say?"

"She says I tried to control her. That I don't respect her."

His mother gave him a long look. "Was she right?" she said evenly.

"Of course I respect her!" Jackson said, his voice getting hot. Then he looked at his mom. "Sorry," he mumbled.

"Well, that was a yes," Emmie said, returning to her crust to add a little more ice water. "You are a control freak. What else do you expect, growing up the way you did? With what I let…"

His mother paused, frozen mid-stroke in her

crust rolling. This was what she did to get a hold of herself when she got emotional in front of her son. He knew to let it pass.

At last, she put down her rolling pin. She said, "You had a more chaotic upbringing than I would have liked for you, Jackson, and yes, that has helped to shape you. You've turned most of those experiences into strengths, but control in relationships is dangerous. So you screwed up. Big deal. So fix it. You've worked so hard to become the man you are, and you should be proud of that, but what on earth makes you think that you're *done*?"

Jackson looked at her like she'd just told him the meaning of life. At that moment, she had. He leapt up and kissed his mother on the cheek.

Emmie picked up her rolling pin, hiding a satisfied smile. "Have you told her about any of this? About your dad?"

"No, that's the last thing I wanted to do if she was scared."

If Jackson expected his mother to understand this particular reasoning, he was disappointed. Emmie rolled her eyes. "Christ, what a dummy."

Jackson let out a surprised laugh.

"Ava called me a asshole."

"Ha! She was right. Now get me some butter from the freezer," she said, frowning down at the dough. "This batch is not, unfortunately, destined for greatness. Good thing I can always try again, huh?"

His mother looked very pleased with that last line.

"*Touché*, Mom," Jackson smiled. "Anything for

me to eat while you conjure up another pie crust?"

He was suddenly voraciously hungry. It was the first time he'd actually wanted food in nearly a week.

For the next several hours, Jackson wolfed down pieces of pie, pastries, and a whole bunch of things he couldn't pronounce, and dutifully filled out comment cards for his mother's websites on all of them. But his mind was at work while his body was otherwise occupied. He kept getting flashes of Ava, of things she'd said. They still made him wince, some of them, but he knew he was working something out.

What his mom has said kept banging around inside his head, too. *You're not done, Jackson*. He had made so many choices in his life because of Ava, he'd felt *able* to make those choices because of Ava, and yet, he had hidden that fact from her. He owed the man he had become to Ava Barnett, and he had the actual, physical proof of that in his apartment, and he'd literally hidden it in his closet. He always thought it was to keep from spooking her, but maybe that was just a rationalization. Maybe he was just as scared and messed up as she was.

And he did owe her an explanation, on top of everything else. But how could he possible explain all of this? Hell, he wasn't sure he could convince her to take his phone calls ever again; she sure as hell hadn't taken them yet.

What could he possibly...

"Oh shit," he said, leaping up from his chair.

"Language."

"Sorry, Mom, I just...I gotta make a phone call," he said, ham-handing his phone. He paced while he waited for her to pick up. "Lillian? Yeah, I'm coming back tomorrow morning. There's something I need for the launch. You know the Moreau?"

"Of course," Lillian said.

"Send it back. I have a different idea."

chapter 22

At a loss about what to do with a broken door and not wanting to stay at a place that no longer felt like home anyway—if it ever had—Ava called her sister. Together, the two women managed to move everything of immediate importance into Ellie's living room out in Brooklyn, and Ava put the rest in temporary storage.

"What's your roommate going to say?" Ava finally asked. She walked in circles around Ellie, who had collapsed on the couch. Ava felt like if she stopped moving, she'd have to think, and that was the last thing she wanted to do. There were too many dangerous thoughts lurking in her mind like giant, menacing icebergs, just waiting to sink her.

"About that," Ellie said slowly. "You can have the spare room. It's an office right now, but it's got a futon, and you can set up your easel."

Ava looked around. There were two bedrooms. "The spare room?"

"So, Colette isn't my roommate," Ellie said. "She's my girlfriend."

Now Ava sat down.

"What?"

Ellie cocked her head. "You don't have, like, a *problem*...?"

"What? No, I just...how did I not know this?"

Ellie scrunched her feet up on the couch and picked at a thread coming out of her sock. She looked just like Ava did when she got uncomfortable. "None of us are so good at sharing personal stuff, Ava," she said. She meant the Barnett women. "I was going to tell you at dinner. I told Mom. It's not a big deal."

"Not a big deal?" Ava said incredulously.

"Does it have to be?"

Ava thought about this. No, obviously, it wasn't itself a big deal to her, but suddenly finding out there was this whole side you never knew about to someone you love, someone you're supposed to know...

Ava couldn't miss how that particular insight might be relevant to her own life, but she couldn't quite go there yet, even in her own mind. *Thar be icebergs*, she thought, and looked up to find Ellie staring at her with big, scared eyes.

"I didn't mean to lie to you, it just..." Ellie said, trailing off.

Ava sighed, and reached for her sister's hand. "I think I actually get that part. I just can't believe I didn't see it."

Now Ellie smiled. "Ava Barnett's famous sixth sense," she said. "Yeah, how'd that work out for you, mind reader? You didn't see that one coming?"

"Shut up."

"You know, you do have blind spots with some people."

"That's pretty obvious at the moment," Ava said.

"No, but I mean it," Ellie said, extending herself across the couch with her feet in her sister's lap. She was noticeably more comfortable now than she had been just a moment ago. *I guess coming out will do that*, Ava thought, secretly shaking her head.

"You have a pretty big blind spot when it comes to Mom, too. No, Ava, listen, please," Ellie said. Ava had stiffened immediately. "You're great and perceptive with people, and you adapt immediately and just charm the pants off them because you see right through them—I know. I've always envied it, even though I know you got it from having to predict when Mom would fly off the handle, which actually sucks pretty hard. But I feel like that's led you to think that you see *everything*, and you just don't."

"I'm actually pretty aware that I don't see everything, El," Ava said softly. "After today."

Ellie winced. Ava hadn't offered details about what had happened, and Ellie hadn't asked, in the great reflexive Barnett tradition of Not Talking About It, but Ellie had seen the busted up door.

"Do you want to talk about it?" Ellie asked.

"Not yet."

"Ok." Ellie put an affectionate foot on Ava's shoulder, just to gross her out. "I'm right about Mom, though."

"Ellie, seriously. You didn't take the brunt of it.

I'm not saying that to, like, pull rank, but—"

"But you are. Shut up for a second, seriously, and listen to me." Ellie got on her knees, leaned forward, and grasped Ava by the sides of her face. Ava was so startled that she actually did shut up.

"You are Mom's favorite. Don't argue with me, and don't think it's something I'm upset about. I'm only saying it because you still think Mom was, like, I don't know, trying to destroy you, with all the stuff she did. I don't think she was. I think she was desperate, and lonely, and drunk, and she would get afraid of losing you, too, every time she lost anyone else, and she just... I think she just wanted to keep you close, as fucked up as that is."

Ava didn't know what to say. Ellie fell back on her side of the couch, somehow spent, as though she'd been waiting to say that for a long time.

Ellie looked shyly at her sister. "Don't say anything, don't... I mean, you don't have to agree with me. Just please think about it, ok? As, like, an option."

"As an option," Ava agreed, still mildly stunned. There had been a whole lot of revelations and surprises for one day. She was suddenly exhausted.

"Sleepy?" Ellie asked.

"God, yes," Ava said. She put her head in her hands. "Oh shit. I didn't call my boss."

Ava had no intention of going into work the next day, or possibly even the day after that. It was the week between Christmas and New Year's, so it wasn't as though it mattered much, but Ava had been pretty absentee lately.

Ellie eyed her thoughtfully. "That isn't like

215

you."

"I *know*."

The strange sense of apathy that Ava had started to associate with her job while up at the Volare estate had only intensified, if that was something apathy could do. It had definitely grown. Expanded. The past day, with Jackson and thinking about painting and all the rest, had put the whole thing into even sharper focus, making her advertising executive ambitions seem even more alien and insane. She realized she wouldn't care at all if she never worked in advertising again. It was like figuring out you'd been wearing the wrong size shoes for years, and that's why nothing had ever felt right. She waited for the requisite terror that was supposed to follow the thought that one was on the verge of becoming unemployed, especially given the economy, and had no explanation when it didn't arrive. She decided to send Alain an email claiming her remaining vacation days, but other than that, she had no idea what she was going to do.

But God, did she prefer thinking about that to thinking about Jackson.

Ava did lots of things to avoid thinking about Jackson. The first thing she did was give custody of her phone to her sister.

"I am not to be trusted," she explained. The shock of the breaking in incident had worn off, and though Ava was still completely messed up about him, that didn't stop her from wanting him. Even thinking about Jackson sent her into a mildly crazed state, confused between desire, love, hurt, and possibly some other things, too. She did not want to be getting phone calls, or worse, have to wonder why she *wasn't* getting phone calls.

So Ava spent a quiet week with Ellie and Colette, eagerly getting to know this side of her sister's life. She was both delighted and a little incredulous to find that they seemed to have a totally functional, happy, and loving relationship, and realized that she still didn't quite believe such things existed, at least not for anyone in her family. And yet, here was the proof. Every night over dinner, there it was. Her sister and even her mother had apparently managed it. Ava had never been so happy for Ellie, but it made her feel her own failings more acutely.

During the days, though, Ellie went to her job as an assistant art director at an off-Broadway theater, Colette went to go do whatever it was that lawyers did, and Ava painted. She hadn't had a plan when she'd started, she'd just kind of…started.

And it turned out that her first painting was of her mother.

"Huh," Ava said.

It had been painted from memory, and it was full of soft light. It was a far more gentle, caring sort of picture than Ava had thought herself capable of producing where Patricia Barnett was concerned.

She painted portraits of Ellie, of Colette. She tried to paint a portrait of herself, but stopped when she started to cry. She wasn't there yet.

She didn't try to paint Jackson. She couldn't handle that yet, either. She already knew what it would show: she was in love with him, she hated him, and she was afraid, if not of him, then of what he made her feel. Not that it mattered. Someone with Ava's past couldn't possibly make it work with someone who had such a tendency to push past every boundary he saw, with someone who withheld so much while demanding even more.

He wasn't abusive—he didn't take it that far, and seemed aware of where that line was—but...but Ava didn't think she could handle it, not yet. Jackson had talked about how much he'd changed over the years, and Ava—Ava hadn't, because she hadn't. She obviously had some issues to work out before she was ready for anyone, let alone Jackson. Well, she assumed. It wasn't like he'd confided in her, either. She had to think it couldn't work as long Jackson Reed remained a black box of mystery.

She'd been thinking about that man for ten years, and had next to nothing to show for it. There was something profoundly unfair about being indelibly tied to someone you couldn't have because you were never quite ready for each other.

Or maybe it wasn't that. Maybe she just wasn't right for him. After all, if he felt he could truly be himself with her, the way he'd asked her to be with him, wouldn't he have actually just *done* it? Wouldn't he have confided in her, too? Shown that he trusted her?

Or maybe he was just an irreparably screwed up jerk.

Ava would torture herself with such thoughts, then remember that she was trying to give herself a break, and move on to something else. But the thoughts always returned. She always circled back around to Jackson, as though anchored to him.

It sucked.

So Ava was actually relieved when Ellie announced that they were going to a New Year's Eve party, and Ava was coming whether she wanted to or not.

"I'm gonna doll you up," Ellie said. "It'll be fantastic."

"Where is it?" Ava hadn't been *out* out in a while.

"Some artsy fartsy fashionable thing in SoHo," Ellie said vaguely. "One of Colette's clients got us in. Now, let's talk about what you're going to wear."

Aware of Ava's highly tuned social sensitivity, Colette waited until Ava was off in the other room trying on clothes before shooting Ellie an inquisitive, confused look.

"So where did my client get us in?" she asked.

"Shush," Ellie said. "It's a surprise."

"I'll bet."

chapter 23

Jackson wasn't used to nervousness. Even before big meetings with prospective investors, even at the very beginning of ArTech, when he was a nobody trying to convince millionaires to give him money, he'd never been a ball of nerves. He'd been sure of himself and his ideas, and had known that would be enough.

Now, in the middle of this giant party he was throwing for his now-successful company, he wasn't sure of anything. Except that if he put his hand out, it might actually shake. The whole jittery, mind-racing, sweaty feeling was new to him.

It sucked.

He should be able to enjoy the spectacle. Arlene had really outdone herself in every possible sense, and so had whoever was responsible for...well, whatever the hell was going on around him. There were performance art pieces going on periodically, there would be some band from Brooklyn in a little bit, there were models covered in silver paint for some unknown reason walking around with trays of champagne flutes. Everywhere people were drinking and composing art poems and messages and all kinds of things on the touchscreen stations they had set up around the transformed loft office space. All the computers and desks had been banished to a supply room and art and lights decorated the suddenly vast space.

He really should be enjoying this. Feeling nervous was terrible. Was this what it was like for other people all the time? All the ways in which dominance permeated his personality did nothing to help him here. At some point in a healthy D/s relationship, the point where the submissive's consent was even more explicitly necessary, dominance and submission inverted themselves: the submissive held the power, the dominant asked for it, and the two were forever twinned in a symmetry he found beautiful.

He was at that point, though being there made it seem less beautiful and noble, or whatever he'd imagined, and more wretched and torturous. Ava held him in the palm of her hand more so now than she ever had before.

So where the hell is she?

Ellie had promised to bring her. Ava's little sister had seemed genuinely excited about this, which made Jackson feel a little better. At least one other person thought this was a good idea.

"Jackson!"

He turned, not expecting anyone to bother him in the corner he'd picked as an observation point. He was really only interested in one person's arrival, and this wasn't her. It was Lillian.

"Great job, Lillian," he said, referring to the party, the launch—all of it. She swayed as she waved off the compliment. Was she drunk? Jackson wasn't sure he'd ever seen Lillian James drunk.

"What, this old thing?" she said. "What are you doing over here, Jackson? Are you...are you *hiding?*"

"No."

"You look like you're hiding."

"How many of those glasses of champagne have you had?" he laughed.

"Three. Maybe four. But I didn't have time to eat dinner. Listen," she said, dropping her lashes and smiling. "We should be celebrating."

"We are celebrating."

"No, I mean *celebrating*," she said, and then she was on him before he could jump back. Lillian didn't waste any time at all; she went in for a kiss and grabbed at his crotch all at once. And as she did it, Jackson looked over her shoulder and saw Ava Barnett.

~ ~ ~

Ava's suspicions had been slowly, steadily awakening throughout the seemingly endless journey from Park Slope to SoHo. Ellie seemed to get vaguer and vaguer about the details of where they were going, and Colette stared unhelpfully out the window of their cab.

They were up to something.

Ava's apprehensions were temporarily soothed

by the unbelievable crush of people crowding around their destination. They all looked young and beautiful and hip, most of them drunk and smoking, all of them flirting with someone, even if it was just themselves, and it really did seem like exactly what Ellie had first described to her: some artsy fartsy fashionable thing. Which was perfect. Ava's ban on thinking about serious things was still very much in effect, and none of the people who crowded into the elevator with them and smushed Ava against the back wall looked like they would require her to think in order to make conversation. She hadn't even had the courage to ask Ellie if Jackson had called, though she was finally at the point where she could admit that she really, really, really wanted him to have called. She just didn't know what she wanted to say to him.

It's New Year's Eve, Ava. Do not go down that rabbit hole. Try to have fun.

And as soon as the elevator doors opened directly on the party, as they always did in those old loft buildings, Ava was in heaven. It was like an interactive, drunken, beautiful art show all around her.

"Dude," she said to Ellie. Ellie just smiled and grabbed her hand.

"Come on," she said.

They got about five feet before a man stepped directly in Ava's path.

Alain? Are you kidding me? Of course he'd be at a party like this.

"Ava!" he said, and extended his arms. The man was wearing a cravat and still somehow managed to leer at her. "You have been very bad, not

223

answering my calls! Listen, we must talk about serious things—"

"Oh God, Alain, I quit."

Ellie slowly turned her head to stare at her sister. Alain simply stood still and blinked. Ava did a quick inventory and found no feeling of panic or impulse, just...relief. Profound, profound relief.

"No, really," she said. "I don't care if this is stupid. I'm not right for this job, and I'm not going to sleep with you. I quit."

"Ava?" Ellie said.

"Nope, it's really ok. I know, I know—no big decisions after—" Ava had almost said 'after a break up,' but couldn't quite do it. She pushed ahead. "But seriously, just—I quit. Have a nice year, Alain, I hope to never see you again. Come on, Ellie."

She dragged Ellie over to a gorgeous, silvery statue that held a tray of champagne flutes, grabbed one, and slugged it down.

"Holy crap, Ava, that was awesome."

"I know, right? I hope I don't feel nauseous in like five minutes," Ava said. She had a definite adrenaline rush going, a kind of buzz, and she was pretty sure it came from feeling like she'd made an actual good decision. It might not necessarily have been the responsible choice, but it had been the right one. It thrilled her like almost nothing else.

That thrill lasted about thirty seconds, and then Ava saw a giant sign announcing "ArtLingua."

Jackson's company.

This was Jackson's *party*.

"Ellie," she said very low. Ellie probably didn't even hear her, but she didn't need to; she saw

Ava's face.

"Please don't be mad," Ellie begged. "You have to give him a chance to at least explain. I'm pretty sure you're avoiding him for the wrong reasons, but at the very least, closer right? Please? Go on, hear him out, and then if you wanna leave, we leave, and I promise to never, ever, ever try to look out for you ever again."

Ava looked sharply at her very sincere sister, but couldn't sustain it. Ellie had always had Ava wrapped around her finger. Ava sighed. "When did you get so good at this life coaching thing? Or guilt trips—whichever one this is."

"I don't know, but it's pretty great. I mean, it only works on other people, obviously. I think it's Colette's influence. She is wise." Ava saw Ellie's face light up as she spied her girlfriend trying to interact with some sort of mime on the other side of the room. "Except now she's had a glass of champagne, so if I don't get over there soon, she's gonna start trying to buy stuff, and we do *not* have room. Not with all the stuff of yours that we're gonna put on the walls," Ellie said, and skipped away before Ava could correct her on that particular point.

"Go find him," Ellie shouted over the din as she walked away. "Promise!"

Not like Ellie waited for a response. Little sisters: the best kind of pain in the ass.

But Ava could only shake her metaphorical fist at Ellie for so long before the reality of her surroundings intruded. She really was at Jackson Reed's New Year's Eve launch party. Her little sister did have a point about Ava being scared.

And being scared was maybe the worst reason to avoid taking chances. Being scared felt distressingly familiar to Ava, and the urge to hide somewhere was uncomfortably compelling, even while the party raged around her. She could run. She could slip into her old disguise, become an unassailable, guarded charmer, pretend that she was really here to enjoy the party. Or she could suit up, find Jackson, and take a chance.

I already quit my job and insulted my boss. I'm on a roll — why not?

So she went in search of Jackson.

And she found him, hidden away in a corner, with that Lillian woman draped all over him.

"No," Jackson said as he locked eyes with Ava. He looked skyward and said, "Just...*why?*"

With great care, he peeled Lillian off of him. Ava could see now that the usually glacial Lillian was, in fact, pretty drunk. Despite the circumstances, it humanized her. Ava wasn't even pissed, though that might have had something to do with Jackson's expression.

"Lillian, I don't want to embarrass you, but this not our relationship, and you know that. You're just kinda drunk. We'll laugh about it tomorrow, I promise, but right now..." He looked at Ava. Belatedly, so did Lillian. "I have something important to attend to," Jackson finished.

Ava waved.

"Oh, come on," Lillian finally said, rolling her eyes and stumbling a little, as though her body tried to follow the gesture. "Can't take a joke anymore. No fun at all."

And she staggered off, the combination of

drunkenness and her usual regal bearing cutting a path in the crowd before her.

"Ava, I swear—" Jackson said vehemently.

"I believe you," Ava said. "Trust me, there was some unsexy body language going on there."

They smiled at each other and then fell into an awkward silence, which was made no better by the sounds of the party all around them. Ava couldn't stop looking at him, wondering if she'd ever see him again after this moment, wondering if he'd kiss her, wondering if she was making a huge mistake. She was seized by a powerful need for him right then, her body suddenly remembering everything it had experienced at his hand, and she stumbled a little with the effort of restraining herself. Their eyes locked again, and she knew, the way she so often knew with Jackson, that he was feeling the same thing.

"Oh God," she mumbled. She felt lost already.

He reached for her hand, but she pulled back. She said, "I don't think I can handle it if you touch me, Jackson. I won't… I need to think clearly. Why am I here?"

The sadness in his eyes when she pulled her hand away was almost unbearable, but he nodded. She felt that he understood. He fumbled for a second, saying, "I wrote this down, I swear…" But after a few seconds, he gave up in frustration. He swore. "Look, Ava, I suck at this stuff, but I'm gonna try, ok? I'm gonna try to explain, but it would be easier if I could just show you. I need you to come with me. Will you follow me? No funny stuff, I promise."

Ava was regretting not taking his hand, not

being able to touch him, not being alone with him. What did it matter? She already wasn't thinking clearly. When he'd said no funny stuff, her heart sank. She was a mess. Hearing what he had to say might be her only way back to sanity. If it were something awful, something inadequate, she'd know right then and there that this was just a physical addiction she needed to get over. She could handle that.

She nodded. "Ok."

Jackson led her through the throng of drunk hipsters, muscling people aside when necessary. The crowd had gotten thicker and rowdier, even in the last fifteen minutes. It was already hot, and people were beginning to sweat. By the time midnight came around, the place would be insane.

Jackson reached a roped off wrought-iron staircase, leading to the off-limits lofted area above, which was guarded by a huge, silent man with a t-shirt that read "Security." Jackson looked back just as some bright young thing careened into Ava, hard. He reached out and caught Ava just as she began to fall and pulled her close, nearly lifting her off the ground with his arm hooked around her waist. He held her pressed against him, and neither of them moved.

Ava's heart thudded in her chest. Every nerve in her entire treacherous body screamed for Jackson. That arm around her waist set fire to her core, her blood thumping in her clit like it had its own pulse.

"Oh shit," she said aloud.

"I'm sorry," he said. But they both knew he didn't entirely mean it, and he didn't let her go.

"Please," she begged. She almost wanted to cry.

This wasn't fair. Jackson took one look at her face and released her, and they both tried to catch their breath.

"Will you still—?"

"I promised," she said.

He removed the rope, and they climbed the stairs in silence.

The lofted area above the party was dark, and the noise of the party felt as though it were coming from far away. The feeling of being alone, together, descended upon Ava much too quickly. She wasn't prepared, and she found herself afraid to speak for fear of what she might say, and afraid to move for fear of what she might do.

Jackson looked at her and saw that she was paralyzed. This time, he took her hand.

"Ava, look," he said, and pointed below.

On the far side of the loft from the entrance, on a central, raised sort of stand, stood the portrait that Ava had painted of Jackson on that night ten years ago when he had broken her heart.

Ava stared at it dumbly, not knowing what to think or feel. The sight of it brought back everything from that night, from the way she'd discovered how she felt about him, truly felt, as she painted, to the disbelieving joy she'd felt when he kissed her, to how alone and broken she'd known herself to be when she'd told him her darkest fantasy and he'd only looked at her in horror.

Jackson was grinning, but there was sweat on his forehead. "All of New York is gonna think I'm one egotistical S.O.B., putting my own portrait up like that."

"Why did you?" Her own voice sounded tinny,

hollow.

Jackson took a deep breath.

"Because that is the reason I owe you everything," he said. "Look at that portrait, Ava. You painted me as…just *look* at it. You made me look kind, and gentle, and… Look, no one had ever—man, *I'd* never even thought of myself that way." Jackson made a strangled noise, and Ava was surprised to see he was trying not to tear up. "This is going be hard to explain, but I'm just going to go with it."

She squeezed his hand. The current that always ran between them surged, and it seemed to propel him forward with his story.

"That picture might look ordinary to you, Ava, but holy God, did it get me through some stuff. My daddy was a mean, drunk, violent man, and he used to beat the shit out of my mother and me. I mean, he really… She still has a limp. She'd kick him out, he'd come back, and there wasn't anything we could do. And when I say 'mean,' I mean I think the man was truly evil. He could be charming, and she only married him to get away from home…but that doesn't matter. 'Son of a bitch dick dad' is the long and short of it. And I was terrified—*terrified*, Ava—that I was gonna be like him."

"Jackson—"

"No, let me finish, please. I've never told anyone this, and I don't want to clam up again before I get it all out."

Ava had never seen him like this, and she was pretty sure no one ever had. One hand gripped the railing in front of them with white-knuckled fury, his whole body wired with tension. Only the hand that held hers looked gentle. She squeezed it again, and nodded.

Jackson set his jaw and started talking again.

"I wasn't just terrified I was going to be like him, I was terrified I *was* like him, deep down, and there wasn't anything I could do about it. I knew for a long time what I wanted in the bedroom, and Ava, holy shit, it scared me. I thought I was a goddamn monster. I thought the best thing I could do was just stay away from all women. I thought about the *seminary*, for Chrissake, and I'm not even Catholic. Just to…"

"And then you painted that picture, Ava. I don't even remember how we got into it, you deciding to paint my portrait, do you?"

She shook her head. "It just seemed…"

"Right. Yeah. It just seemed…inevitable. You painted this picture that looked like me, but…it was like you saw something completely different in me. Like I was good. Like I wasn't a monster. Every moment with you was like that, Ava," he said fiercely, turning now to face her completely, grabbing her other hand. He stared into her face, like he was determined to have this one moment when they faced nothing but each other, when he was totally bared to her, as she had once been to him.

"Do you get that?" he asked her. "Every moment with you, the way you just seemed to understand me, I got a little better at seeing myself through your eyes, and believing I could be different. That maybe there was something in me worth…"

231

He stopped, unable to finish that last sentence. Ava was stunned. It had never once occurred to her that the understanding and connection she felt from Jackson might have been reciprocal, and been just as important to him. She'd just taken it for granted that she'd needed him more than he'd needed her, and she been on her guard because of it.

"Anyway," he said. "Then that night, when you told me you wanted to be tied up—I mean, shit, Ava, it was our first time together!"

Ava said very quietly, "I might have been overly exuberant."

"It just made me think…I don't know, I freaked out, and I took it out on you with my attitude, and by the time I figured out how dumb I was being, it was too late. All I had left was that painting. So…I kept it. That painting, Ava, has been like a beacon for me. Actual, real, physical evidence that someone believed in me as much as you did. I just worked toward it, these past ten years."

Jackson paused. He let go of one hand and hesitated, just for a second, which was so unlike him, and then the familiar, dominant posture was back, and he put his hand on her cheek, his fingers threading through her hair, and wrapped his other arm around her waist.

"I do not exaggerate when I say this, Ava, so listen very, very carefully: everything I am today, I've become because of you. For you. For right now, this moment, when I can tell you that I love you, that I've always loved you, that I always will, and that I am not *done* becoming the man you deserve. I fucked up horribly, Ava, and I never should have hidden any of this from you, and I will probably fuck up again, but I promise you, *promise* you, that I will never stop trying. I promise you—"

"Shut up," she said, and her voice cracked.

Jackson opened his mouth, then closed it again, speechless for the first time.

She said very quietly, "I'm not entirely sure I deserve you, either."

For the first time that night, Jackson smiled a big, gleaming, boyish smile. "Shut up," he said.

And he kissed her.

epilogue

Jackson surveyed his company's office space with supreme satisfaction. Once more it had been turned into a gallery, but a better one this time. It was Ava's first show.

So, of course, she was hiding up in the loft.

She'd made it all of ten minutes before the anxiety of putting her work—her *self*, as she had explained impatiently—on display, and for actual sale, had become too much for her. She'd been determined to experience all of this without resorting to her usual defenses, but it was proving more difficult than she'd thought.

"Either I get five minutes in the loft, or I lose my mind," she'd said when he had begged her not to miss out. "You stay here, and make sure...I don't even know. Make sure nothing gets set on fire."

And then she'd fled.

Which is why she had no idea that she'd already sold three portraits and been commissioned for two more. Arlene's boyfriend, Charles Borsa, was handling it. Borsa had been as amazed as anyone at Ava's hidden talent, her weird genius in painting people not necessarily as they appeared, but as they were. She used a bunch of styles to do it—all of them beautiful, in Jackson's opinion. She'd actually gotten better since college.

And she was freaking out up in the loft. That wasn't right. She deserved triumph, and he knew she could handle it. And Jackson didn't want anything to sully this day, in particular.

She needed to relax. Jackson's plans could be brought forward a couple of hours for that. He was a flexible guy. He went and got the package he'd hidden in his office and went up to the darkened loft.

Ava was there, all the way in the back, sitting in the shadows on an old packing crate with her knees bunched up around her. Her fingers drummed nervously on her knees, but as soon as Jackson approached, she had questions.

"Do they like them? Oh God, they don't. Have any of them sold? No, don't tell me, it's fine. It's ok. I can always do something else. I don't—"

"Quiet," he said in his Dom voice. He loved watching her snap to attention like that. "You have sold three portraits. You have been commissioned for two more. The word 'genius' is being thrown around a lot, which, I'm going to point out, means I've been right the whole time."

She put her legs down and leaned forward. "You're not *always* right." She grinned at him. "Wait, really?"

"Yes, really."

She giggled, then covered her mouth and tried to look dignified. "I feel like such an idiot."

"You are an idiot right now. An adorable, beautiful, lovable idiot. And I'm going to take full advantage of your temporary idiocy." Jackson produced a little package, which he'd been hiding behind his back. It was a small, unassuming pastry box. He was trying very, very hard not to shake.

"Is that what I think it is?" she asked, taking it from him with a big smile.

"Probably not."

Ava frowned and opened the box. It was, as she'd expected, a red velvet cupcake with buttercream icing. The surprising part was the diamond solitaire ring poised on a whip of icing.

"Oh my God," she whispered.

Jackson's stomach was doing flip-flops, something he remembered as a symptom of nervousness. He preferred to think it was adrenaline. Adrenaline, definitely. Christ, why hadn't she said anything?

"Ava?"

She popped the ring in her mouth.

In all the many ways Jackson had played this out in his mind, he'd never, ever, ever thought about what to do if she ate the damn ring.

"Ava?" he said again, this time with bewilderment.

Ava's cheeks hollowed out briefly, and then she took the ring out, now clean of icing, and slipped it on her finger. "Yes, you dummy," she said shyly. "Now please kiss me before I start crying."

Jackson did more than that. He pulled her to her feet, kissed her thoroughly, and unzipped the back of her dress.

"Jackson!" Ava laughed.

He put one finger under her chin and tilted her face back up to his. Then he slipped her shoulder straps down, and the dress fell to the floor. "That wasn't just a proposal, sweetheart," he said, grinning. "It was also an order."

She smiled, shivering as he ran his hands over her naked breasts and then bent to pull off her panties. "Yes sir," she said.

ABOUT THE AUTHOR

Chloe Cox writes erotic romance, steamy romance, paranormal romance…just, really, any kind of romance, from a secret bunker in the middle of nowhere. Well, no, not really. She lives in a normal house, even if it is a bit messy. She can be found most readily at her website, chloecoxwrites.com, or Facebook or Goodreads, or her trusty old email address, <u>chloe@chloecoxwrites.com</u>.

Made in the USA
Lexington, KY
31 August 2013